The Journey To Mount Kailash

by

Robert Leach

INDIGO DREAMS PUBLISHING

First Edition: The Journey To Mount Kailash

First published in Great Britain in 2010 by:
Indigo Dreams Publishing
132 Hinckley Road
Stoney Stanton
Leics
LE9 4LN
www.indigodreams.co.uk

Robert Leach has asserted his right under the Copyright, Designs and Patents Act 1988 to be identified as the author of this work.
©2010 Robert Leach

ISBN 978-1-907401-22-0

British Library Cataloguing in Publication Data. A CIP record for this book can be obtained from the British Library.

This book is sold subject to the condition that it shall not, by way of trade or otherwise, be lent, re-sold, hired out, or otherwise circulated without the author's and publisher's prior consent in any form of binding or cover other than that in which it is published and without a similar condition including this condition being imposed on the subsequent purchaser.

Designed and typeset in Times New Roman by Indigo Dreams.

Cover design by Ronnie Goodyer at Indigo Dreams.

Printed and bound in Great Britain by Imprint Academic, Exeter.

To Joy

Fellow traveller, artist, critic, friend

'India is more than a country; India is also an idea.'

To cull contentment upon wildest shores,
And luxuries extract from bleakest moors ...

WILLIAM WORDSWORTH
Memorials of a Tour in Scotland, 1803

The Journey to Mount Kailash

Contents

List of illustrations	ii
List of maps	ii
Acknowledgements	iii
1 : Because	2
2 : Beginning	10
3 : A False Move	36
4 : The Song of South India	51
5 : Still Life	80
6 : The Snake Uncoils	117
7. At Last	174
Notes	201

Illustrations

Divali in Kochi	15
The Nut Man	26
Madurai Temple towers covered in coconut leaves	50
Krishna's butter-ball, Mamallapuram	55
Arjuna's Penance	57
Theyyam performance, near Kunnur, Kerala	68
Rangoli: Vaikom Elephant Festival	73
Elephants, fire, a brilliantly lit arch, crowds of people	76
Sunderbans	83
Park Street cemetery, Kolkata	108
Kanchenjunga range (the sleeping old man)	116
Temple at Khajuraho	126
Carving on side of Khajuraho temple	127
Shiva lingum in inner sanctum, temple at Khajuraho	128
Kali dances on Shiva: traditional image	130
Bahadur Shah II 'Zafar'	159
Bahadur Shah II 'Zafar': original Urdu script	169
Nationalist group at Ashoka's Stone	171
Lamayurru monastery, Ladakh	184
Spring Festival at Stok monastery	189
Climax of the spring ceremony at Stok monastery	193
Desert beetle	200

Maps

India – The Journey to Mount Kailash	1
Mount Kailash, Lake Mansarovar and Raksha Tal	6
South India.	52
West and East Bengal	82
The plains of the River Ganga	117
The River Indus	177

Acknowledgements

Several people read *The Journey to Mount Kailash* while it was in the making. For their comments, criticisms, questions and suggestions, I wish to thank them sincerely:

Tom Bryan, Angela Bull, Martin Bull, Vee Freir, Peter Hinchcliffe, Nicholas Leach, Joy Parker, Natasha Singleton, Olga Taxidou, John Topping.

India : The Journey to Mount Kailash

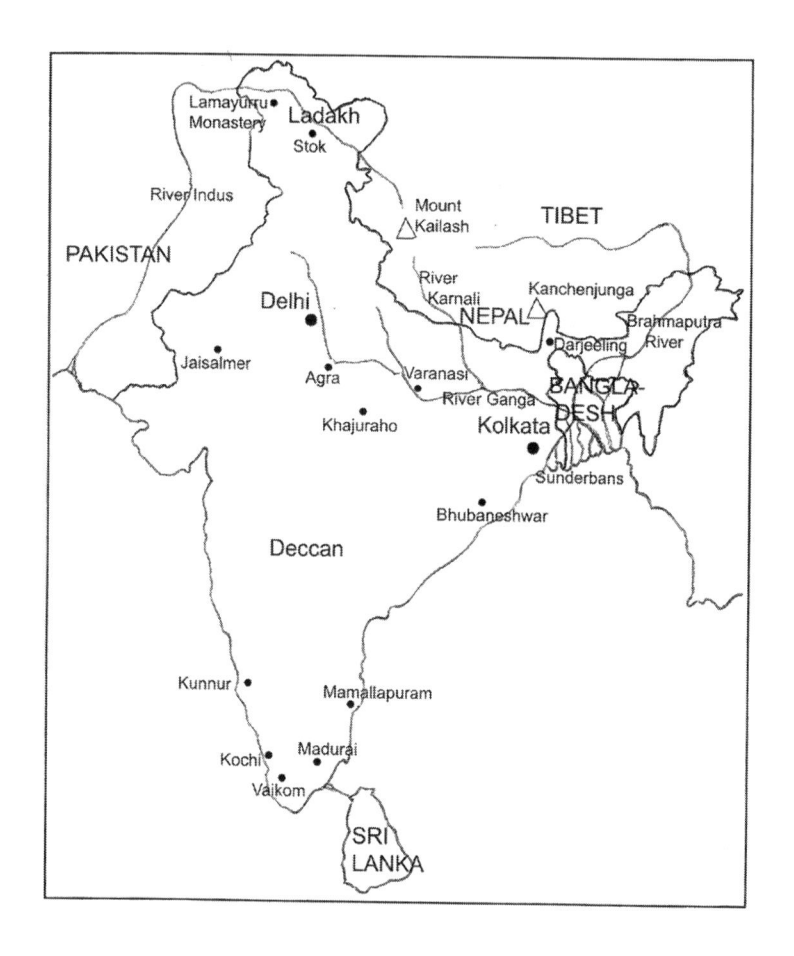

One : Because

In the Darkness

In the darkness before dying
You crouch fearfully,
Remember, and curse.

Time to be honest.
A donkey is not a horse,
And a mule is neither.

Ambitious, and too ambitious,
For forty years I took my match
To the blue touchpaper of success,

And never,
Never sent a rocket
Into the void.

Did I lack daring? Fear
My fireworks would be
Damp squibs, fizzle ... ?

When I moved towards
The wished-for brilliance
Of poetry or songs,

Some stage or actor caught my eye.
I turned aside, allowed myself to be
Entranced by drama, till

An academic problem filched my mind,
Pushed a sparkling box of arguments
At me. But as I gave my mind to

These intellectual jumping jacks,
The next treat in the box –
Pedagogy – tempted me, promised

A bonfire of old ways.
So I turned to it.
And turn and turn about

I spun and fizzed,
Became myself a catherine wheel,
Whizzed and whirligigged

To empty, sputtering end,
Dull in the dark,
Dead afraid.

And love, my love, that too
Dragged me to distraction,
Knotted up a grass rope of anguish.

I scythed my way through love
Like a mower. A wife is a meadow,
Yet wild flowers grow

On the verges, under the hedgerow,
And there you lie
High and hidden. Besides,

The women you regret
Are not, are never, the wives,
Dead or divorced,

But those tender, fleeting others,
Lost and gone,
Because of … because of …

Impatience, lust, bewilderment
And – again – the brilliant distraction
Of what comes next.

The mower slashes whatever grows,
Makes his hay,
Stacks up an outcast's despair.

But now, one last time, I clutch
A young woman, artist, to me,
And now I peer

Into the emptiness,
The weariness of ending,
With a chalk-drawn last rangoli* of hope,

And swear – my old carthorse will plough this field
With a straight furrow,
At last make dull earth teem.

Thrashed with the whips of hope,
With her I will
Make good my self. Together

We will travel,
Take the trail
To her native India,

To redemption, renewal,
And a single, settled destiny:
Mount Kailash.

Asterisks refer to Notes at the end of the text.

Mount Kailash

You see,
The walk round Kailash
Wipes out
A lifetime of sins.

Mount Kailash,
Solitary on the high Gangadise Way,
Stands.
No range round companions it,
No Alps, no Pyranees, Andes
Or Rockies. Himalaya is leagues away.
Kailash stands alone, and high.

Alone in Xizing,
This 'precious jewel of the glacier snows'
Is black, grey, grassless,
A single upthrust of the world's rock crust,
Flat slashes on its silent sides –
Staircase to the sky.

*   *   *   *

And south and west
The holy geometry
Is complete:

Southish lies Lake Mansarovar,
Lake of Brahma*, Hindu Creator.
At full moon, the snow on Kailash
Is caught, turquoise, silver,
In the mirror of Mansarovar.
Here feed fish,
Plankton, water beetles,
Life abundant.
To the west – Raksha Tal,
Ravana's* water, salt-embittered,
Lake of demons, a dead sea, void

Of whatever's quick, whatever
Breathes, grows old.

And between the two,
Traces of workings, a maybe mine,
Which teases the digger with
Gold.

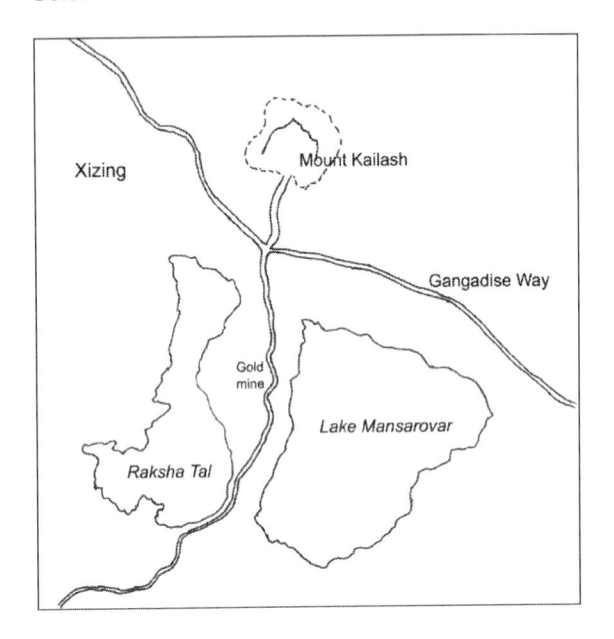

Mount Kailash, with Lake Mansarovar and Raksha Tal.

The sun that shines on snow-mottled Kailash
Gives light, not warmth. The air
Crisps, your lungs
Cringe. The sun slides away.
Quick dusk
Sprays the sky
Indigo, auburn, green,

Purple as wine,
Crimson as blood.

Darkness glows,
Icy winds creep, sweep over Mansarovar,
Bite into bones.
You lie, clenched under rough rocks,
And the freeze storm screeches
Its witch's brew, gobbles up
Your desperation, scours
The barnacles of your belief.

Out of grey, wet, gloomy mist,
The blizzard rears up like a whinnying horse
Shrieking its grief.*

        *   *   *   *

The circumambulation of Mount Kailash
Is 'parikrama' or 'kora'.

The weather doesn't daunt true pilgrims, for
This peregrination procures
Personal merit, psychic powers, nirvana
Perhaps.

Parikrama lasts
Four days – a dozen
Kilometres a day.
Not much?
But the air is thin, the wind
Spite-bladed, you must pitch tents,
Cook up broth, and sleep.

If you learn 'Lung-gom',
The skill of breath, you can keep going,
Circle the mountain
In just a day.

Or, do the opposite. At every step,
Or every few, lay your body in the snow,
Hands stretching to Mount Kailash.
Dig your fingers in the crisp of it, then crawl
To the mark, stand, do the obeisance of the meek,
Walk on a few paces, then
Prostrate yourself again.
This kora may last for weeks.

Mount Kailash,
Pure as a white swan,
Perfect as the perfect lotus,
Centre of the universe,
Incarnation of eternal power,
Mystic meeting point of earthly opposites.

Medicinal herbs grow here,
Rare snakes, known nowhere else, are seen.
But the unwary botanist or serpent-seeker
Needs beware:
Huge hungry dogs patrol the place,
Attack – no warning, no kind hearts
In this scant air.

Some believe their dead forebears
Dwell in Mount Kailash in eternal peace.
For Bons*, Hindus, Jains
And the Buddhists of Tibet,
This is the destination
Of destinations, the goal of goals,
For all who seek
The cleansing of tired souls.

Here Shiva* sits. Pilgrims relate
How if you concentrate you see
His meditating shape unclose
As perhaps you see
Familiar faces in dying embers,
Or tigers in the sea's foam.

Shiva contemplates the world:
To destroy? To preserve? To create
Something else, something new?
Shiva, destroyer and restorer, near and far,
Merges paradox, fuses contradictions,
Yet holds the power to shift
Sun, moon, star.

Some say that
Merely to see the holy mountain
Is enough
To obtain relief,
Release from delusion, ignorance,
Self-disgust, that thus
The darkness before dying
Is lightened, refreshment
Rendered to the soul.

So –
To get to Kailash,
Perhaps perform parikrama –
That's the goal:
And she and I will be
Re-made, whole.

Two : Beginning

Shah Jahan's Feast

1
Where slender-thighed *nautch** girls dance,
Toss their gauzy shifts
To make the candles caper,
Mumtaz murmurs in Shah Jahan's* ear:
Eat
My *murgh**
One mouthful at a time.
Consider
The flavours:
Cloves, cardamom pods, dry-roasted cumin
Which palter and sputter in wheezing pans –
Chicken pieces, lemon-drizzled,
Forked from fat that licks and spits –
And onion, garlic, ginger –
And turmeric, chilli, coriander –
Can you eat all this
In one greedy gobful?

Her laughter wind-chimes
In his ear.

On his tongue
Each taste and tang and flavour and savour
Emerges, submerges,
Merges delights,
Like flowers by the wayside,
Like hours on a journey.

And we must make to Kailash
One foot at a time,
Imbibe

History, legend, story
Like so many spices
To tease and tempt
In the word and in the telling.
To make the meal we feel
We digest these seasonings
Together, apart,
Place, word, act,
And allow
Time
To tread our way.

    2
So to begin:
Bhubaneshwar? City of temples:
We must learn
The shape of Shiva's face.
Bhubaneshawar –
Ancient city of Ashoka's* edict:
We must hear his word. Is this then
Our stepping-off place?

Or Aurangabad?
City of the last great Mughal,
Aurangzeb* the merciless,
In whose time India became
The richest, most cultured civilization
Man had ever managed.

Or Simla? Or Ooty?*
Where white-skinned tyrants,
At peace and at leisure,
Potted reds and colours*
Between sweet, sweaty flirtings
With bored Mrs Hauksbees.*

Cloves, cardamom, cumin, coriander
Spit and fizzle.
Aromas arise.

To taste the musk and scent of India,
To savour its pungency, the relish of its recipe,
Start far from Kailash,
Take one taste at a time.
Our destiny – our *dharma*.*
Start in the south, begin
Where you began –
Kochi
In Malabar*
In Kerala.

Here
Stand – understand – deserve.
Approach slow.
Observe.

Kochi Observed

Fish, Men, Trees

Silver fish, slabbed and waiting
For a buyer;
Men mending blue fishing nets
Hunched in canoes;
Tree roots older than the world,
Twined and intertwined;
And the voice of the boxwallah*
Pedalling his tricycle into the morning:
'Ahoo! Ahoo! Ahoo-eee!'

Pariah Dogs

The night is smudged, grubby.
Yelpings scribble
Over every page.
Sleepily you think:
'Owls? In Kochi?'
But it's the dogs.
'A steamer on the waterway? At this hour?'
But it's the dogs.
'Cock-crow? Already?'
It's the dogs, the dogs.
The corners of night's book
Slowly curl.

Enlightenment

We arrived
The day after the festival
In honour of
Saraswati, goddess of education.
Beautiful, milk white, she still reposed
On her water lily
In our hosts' home-made shrine
And the scent of ghee, incense, aromatic wood
Still lingered.
Before smouldering ashes,
Smoky joss sticks, a scattering of
Marigolds and flames of the forest,
They offered us holy food –
Banana shreds, grapes, puffed rice, tapioca
Mixed to sweet harmony –
And we ate with our right hands
While our left hands covered our heads.
Then we drank to enlightenment.

Our willing warmth in the performing
Seemed stranger than the performance when
A few days later our host confessed
He was a Catholic.

In Kochi are Moslems, Jews, Jains, Chinese.
Does any of that matter?

Dawn

Night cracks
At cock-crow,
So loud, so near
Your sleepy head conjures
A cockerel the size of an ostrich.

A muezzin's call
Hovers in the lazy mist.

Then a mangle of disputatious crows
Improvise bad jazz,
Dogs are shouting,
And the first auto-rickshaw
Grunts awake.

The omelette of day
Begins to cook.

Kali Puja*

Black velvet folds of night;
Prickles of yellow, orange;
Candle flames in every window,
On garden walls, by gateposts, tree trunks ...

A temple veiled in flaring tapers,
A lace shawl of lights; and people
On tiptoe, breathing in;
In shadowed passages, under sheds, beside ghost bridges,
Cuddles of children sit,
Whisper, giggle and the curtained night
Is suddenly ablaze, fired
By sprouting, crackling sparklers
And rockets springing
Into soft black vacancy. Somewhere
A band bangs drums,
And on every doorstep
Rangolis –
Proclaiming holy Divali*.
Just beyond the little lights
Something is there, something.

Divali in Kochi

On the Bus

Palm leaves are kite's wings
Against the silver sky.

Below –
"English as the experts speak it."
"Hope for salvation."
"Best tailors." "Spare tyres."
"Fascination and beauty for women
And gentlemen."

Blue hibiscus, grey canal water,
Glimpse of brick-making.
So many people on the road:
Silk, faces, feet, dust.
So many people in the bus:
Elbows, rucksacks, eyes, rupees,
Just holding their feet with the swaying jousts.
And puddles, saris, a cow or two …

Brakes howl, the bustle bursts –
A motorbike sideways, wheel
Crumpled like paper.
Some people are lifting a man
Gently. His
Limbs are faint-floppy
And blood
Sops his chin and chest.

Then people again, palm fronds,
And the brightness of clothing, posters, sun …

Crab

Lunch: crabmeat scrounged from jaggy shells,
Grilled with cumin and cardamom.

On the foreshore, fishermen lay out their catch
On plastic platters:

Marlin, snapper, mullet, prawn.
Two too-lively crabs

Crawl greedily for the prawn pile.
The babachee* curses with unfathomable fury,

Flings them back
Where they belong.

I bite the brittle claw, its broken edge
Tears my tongue, brings blood.

Bats at Sunset

You don't notice it, but
In half an hour the sky
Dies – blue to pink
To indigo to black.
A star or two, the moon maybe,
Are yellow-silver
In the void, but the palm leaves,
Spread like open hands
Supplicating, are black. Just
One or two evening people
Pass this way, or a bicycle
Trills its bell. Dark
Clasps the world,
Releases bats to flounce and flirt.
At first they're small,

Butterfly-like, flittering and flickering;
Then come the airborne mice, pipistrelles,
Weaving and dashing;
And last, the cruiser bats,
Flying foxes, heads down,
Silently, rhythmically, beating their wings,
And boring on like buzz bombs.

Kerala

Inquisitive as macaques, our eyes
Pry into the simmering curries
Of Keralan life –
The people, their doings and stories.

Darikan and Bhadrikali

Darikan, devil-born, came to Brahma, father of the gods, creator, head godhead.
– I have fasted, worn rags, torn my hair for two weeks. Reward me.
Brahma shook his head and his long locks swayed.
– No.
Three weeks later Darikan came again to Brahma.
– I have stood on one leg with my left arm in the air, and my mouth has touched only water and never a crumb of food, for twenty days. Reward me.
Brahma shook his head and his fuzzy beard dithered.
– No.
Three weeks later Darikan came again to Brahma.

– I have crawled over stones from Rameshwaram to Madurai, and I have prostrated myself in worship of Brahma the Great every five steps. Reward me.
Brahma looked at Darikan and this time he nodded, and his fine twirly moustache trembled.
– Yes, said Brahma, you deserve a reward, devil though you be. You deserve to be made invincible.
– Invincible?
– Yes.
– Unbeatable? Unconquerable? Saved for ever from defeat?
– Yes.
Darikan bounded away, cartwheeling and flip-flopping by turns.
Then he assaulted the gods.
He laid waste the gardens of the first god's palace, and because he was invincible, the first god could only shout at him.
He burned the stored provisions and the storehouses and barns of the second god, and because he was invincible, the second god could only curse him.
He pulled down the chimney, then the roof, then the walls of the third god, and the third god, weeping, sent for Naarada, the messenger.
He charged Naarada:
– Tell Shiva of the destruction being wrought by Darikan the Invincible.
Shiva listened to Naarada, then he was silent, considering.
And after a sombre pause, filled with the mystery of silence, Shiva produced a miracle – Bhadrikali, a slender woman, graceful as a dancer, with dark hair, thick eyebrows and eyes of burnt umber.
With a mighty roar, beautiful Bhadrikali set out after Darikan, and when she caught him, she tugged his shoulder so he spun round to face her.
– Now, she spoke, and her voice was firm but soft, Darikan – stop your destructions, or face my music, and she hummed a melody like a harp on a perfumed terrace at evening.
– Never, replied Darikan.

So they set to, and fought and battled and combated with each other, and the heavens echoed with their sword-clashes and their cries and the noise of their feet as they stamped on the earth, till Bhadrikali stood over Darikan, who had dropped his weapon and so was defenceless.
– Now, she said, and her voice was soft as a breeze in reeds, will you stop your destructions?
– Never.
Darikan spoke through his teeth on the ground, and he trembled so his shoes shivered.
– Then here is my music, said Bhadrikali, raising her sword.
– But I am invincible, said Darikan, though the squeak in his voice showed how terrified he was.
– No more! cried Bhadrikali, and her sword swept down with the noise of a harp string plucked.
And Darikan's head was no longer joined to his body.
Even the earth stopped turning to breathe a sigh of relief.
And Shiva said to Bhadrikali,
– Find the most beautiful place in the world, and I shall give it to you as a reward.
Bhadrikali hesitated no longer than the blink of a peacock's eye, and said,
– Kerala.
Because Kerala is fruitful, its foison uncountable –
    cardamom, pepper, tamarind,
    nutmeg, turmeric, fenugreek,
    star anise, cloves, tapioca
    teak, ebony, calico, rubber, sandalwood
    pineapple, mango, oranges, coconuts
    rice, tea, coffee, cashew
Bhadrikali became the special protector of Kerala.

But she couldn't always hold out against robbers …

The Ballad of Vasco da Gama

In 1497, July,
    Bold Vasco and his crew
Sailed from home in Portugal
    In ships both sound and true.

A fair strong wind, and they skimmed along,
    These hundred and seventy hands.
For three long, dreary endless months
    They never saw beach nor land,

Until they came to the Good Hope cape,
    The sailors' awful fear;
But rounded it with a wester wind –
    What no ship had done before.

Vasco da Gama and his men
    Sailed on into the unknown,
Through the Indian Ocean, the Arabian Sea,
    Their carrack ships were blown.

And now to gain what was their aim –
    Treasure, booty, gold –
They searched these waters for merchant ships,
    And robbed them, poop and hold.

Pirates they were, get what they could,
    By sword or lies or crime;
They boasted: 'The creed we live by's clear –
    Profit every time.'

Came the day when they docked in an Afric port.
    Here Vasco took on board
An expert pilot, Ibn Majid,
    An Arab pirate lord.

He steered them through the choppy waves
    And through the balmy seas,

Until they reached the Malabar coast
   With its stately coconut trees.

The zamorin who ruled this coast,
   He knew how da Gama played:
He paused a bit, thought, didn't agree
   To a concessionary trade.

Rather, he asked these Portuguese
   To pay his country's tax
And thus make sure they'd never face
   Jealous-inspired attacks.

Vasco da Gama surly looked,
   He shifted in his shoes,
And his eye looked left and then looked right,
   Seeking how not to lose.

Discretion being the better part
   Of any sailor's valour,
He nodded, sighed, turned back to his ship,
   His face a deathly pallor.

For Malabar and Travancore
   And Cochin* could, by trade,
Sell cardamom, pepper, ebony, teak
   – His fortune could be made.

He left behind the best business minds
   From among his pirate crew,
And sailed back home (but slow and hard),
   Considering what to do.

In Portugal, Vasco's return
   Was met with high acclaim.
His derring-do, his colonial hopes,
   Brought wealth and power and fame.

For three long years da Gama planned,
    Plotted and worked out ways
To make the people of Malabar
    Also sing his praise.

So twenty ships he fitted out,
    Sailed again for the Good Hope cape,
And reached the coast of Malabar
    Ready to outface fate.

Those business brains he'd left behind
    Were now all dead. Enough
For Vasco da Gama's mountainous rage
    To need no kind of bluff.

First an Arab sailing ship he stopped,
    Fired flaming brands so bright,
Burned children, women, men alive
    – No pity for their plight.

Then came a futile, feigned attempt
    To make a treaty here:
But da Gama's offer to the zamorin
    Was blood and death and fire.

Next day began the bombardment,
    The town was torn and flayed,
Houses burned, temples crashed,
    Everywhere enflamed.

And while the stream of fire still roared,
    da Gama sent men out
To catch the crews of the harboured ships
    Trapped by the blazing rout.

Each captured man was sent to death,
    But first, to make him feared,
He had their noses, ears and hands
    Hacked off. Not one was spared.

These human parts were loaded then
    Into a boat, and sent
Back to the burning, toppling town:
    A statement of intent.

Thus Portugal – and Europe all –
    Started the Indies trade,
And if any questioned how it worked
    Such examples were always made.

The European culture that
    Was brought to Malabar,
Did not just stay where it began,
    But was exported wide and far.

The methods pioneered by great
    Vasco da Gama then
Have been refined, but are still in use
    By superpowerful men.

    *   *   *   *

Mother India, wronged –
But in time
She found renewal, relief,
A new springtime.

How did she emerge
From this European onslaught still alive?
Is there a lesson here? We observe
Some of those (or their descendants) who survive.

People

The Nut Man

With a clatter of spoons
Against cooking pot sides
He arrives. Roast nuts, chick peas,
Savoury and sweet:
He deals in treats.

It's bat-hour.
His little handcart's fairy lights
Cheat night
For flickery minutes
And his secret aromas
Psst to the house tops.

For just a rupee (maybe two)
Kids get
Tooth crackers, salt in tangoes,
Roast warmth.

Then he pushes on, and
We hear his clattery pans
In the next street,
And the next,
And the one beyond that …

While our street is still.

The Nut Man

The Little Boat

Would be matchwood
In any contest with other craft
On this wide waterway.

The blue oars
Dip and drip
In shifting, oil-rainbowed water.
They seem
Small as spoons,

But still – our boatman
Brings us home
Before time.

Jasmine

After the heat
After the dust
And the sweat
Trickling between shoulder blade and armpit,
Thigh and knee joint …
After the fly bites,
The dog shit in piles
On the sidewalk
And the importuning
By trinket pedlars and tuk-tuk* drivers
Under the stewing noontime …
After the exhaustion of the jolting journey,

We return to our home-stay
And Jasmine, gatekeeper,
Attends us.

'Namaste', with palms together.
She has cleaned the room
Emptied the bins
Put out fresh towels
Seen to the laundry.

She is small,
Her sari
Engulfs her slender form,
And her face is thin and dark.
Her eyes carry
The long song of the rivers of India
Which flow and flow, echoing
The way of the centuries –
Women's work
Enabling the world.

Behind a Cooking Pot

Coconut palms, spiky spinifex, moist brambly undergrowth –
A flaunting of succulent foliage ...
The road cannot carry so many
Blaring buses, rickshaws, bikes, businesses ...
The heat hovers and pounces,
A gaudy all-seeing despot ...

But sometimes
Behind a cooking pot,
Its smoky aroma,
You glimpse
A shy shadow
Smile.

Casa Linda

The sky reddens the west
When the fishing smacks come back.
Their catch is laid on slabs
In the sea-front's mortuary-mart.

We bargained for
Two kingfish steaks,
Bore them in triumph
To Casa Linda,
To the best cook in Kochi.

Our luck was in.
No-one else in Kochi seemed to know
Of Casa Linda.
The tables were all empty, the cook
Worked just for us, and we
Dined like diwans.

Afterwards, he and his wife
Sat with us, talked
Philosophy and education,
Politics and history,
While outside the open window
The monsoon spat and spouted
Without let – till, in face of its fury,
And as midnight tiptoed up,
Our cook turned chauffeur,
And we got home – fed
And dry.

Two weeks on, and we bought
A bulbous snapper with red scales,
Floppy tail, and eyes that looked
Sad to be caught …
And returned to Casa Linda.

Our cook took the fish
And conjured the expected feast.
But though again we were
His only guests,
Tonight the chat was flat, conversation
Floundered and flopped.

Wife – in hospital – tummy
Griped, in torment ... friend –
Arm torn in a road crash ...
And business – here –
Failing.

He stood
Looking philosophically out,
Window wide to darkening night.

People passed,
Beams of car lights
Wobbled, but went on.
Somewhere voices –

Singing sweetly
Far away.
The heat lapsed a little.
And since no rain fell,
And our fish was picked
Clean to sharp white bones,
We paid
And made our way away,
Waving to him
At his window.

And now we wonder: if we buy
A third fish,
Shall we take it
To Casa Linda?

Kochi

We see
And ask – how
Does this make the mare dance? Who
Are we now?

Reflection

In the mornings,
After you depart
For your art studio,
Conscientiously
I perform my exercises,
Testing the remaining suppleness
In joints and spine.

Somewhere
A monotonous swish-swish –
A housewife sweeping;
Beyond, stretching like elastic,
The racked screech of a cock.
The heat clamps down on the street
Like a lid.

I sit in my underpants
In the draught of the air conditioner,
Drinking instant coffee
And reading Shakespeare.

'Though woe be heavy, yet it seldom sleeps,
And they that watch see time how slow it creeps.'*

Thus I do not solve
The world's problems,
As such;
Nor do I add to them
Much.

Autumn Monsoon

A sword dance of lightening
Surrounds us;
The thunder – a thousand snooker balls
Released and rolling:

The storm toying with us.

You fold down your umbrella
In case it conducts the lightening,
And the water streams
All over your body.

Physics and Metaphysics

I am watching
A pretty brown-and-white mosquito
Stroll slowly
Down my arm.
It is considering
Menu choices:
The meatiness of my forearm
Versus the delicacy
Of my inner wrist;
While I am debating
Moral rights –
His to bite,
Mine to swat.

The Artist

Bright against obscure,
Clear against dim,
The artist lays on
Layers of paint
Carefully. Carefully
She crafts the picture –
Interior and exterior,
There and here –
While invisible in a bush
The brain fever bird*:
'*H-hi-o, h-hi-o, h-hi-o, h-hi-o.*'

A local pundit
Eyes the work. 'No,'
He pronounces, and points to the dark,
The obscure. 'That colour
Is wrong, that colour

Does not exist
In India.' The artist
Does not argue
And the brain fever bird
Stays invisible in his bush:
'*H-hi-o, h-hi-o, h-hi-o, h-hi-o.*'

On Cherai Beach

Hours later –
Rickshaw hours, ferry hours,
Bus hours –
Time stops:
A picture postcardiac arrest of
Coconut palms, white sands,
Rolling breakers.

I sit under my umbrella
And scan the scene,
The scenery.
Three beautiful women
In beautiful saris –
Gold, plum purple, green-and-yellow –
Parade the beach.
Their hips swing, they
Almost dance.
They are talking, laughing.
High cheeks bones, long fish eyes.

When they are past
I lean forward
To gaze,
And one of them, then three, turn back,
Catch me,
My eye.

They laugh.
Then
I laugh
A little, a bit.

Then
They have passed on.

The Party

All that Keralan day
The heat sat on us
Like a hen on her eggs.

In the evening – the party,
With rum punch
And fish or chicken curry
On the candle-lit verandah.
We had seen,
Admired the pictures
Hanging in the gallery;
Now we talked,
Discussed politics, education,
Arranged marriage, caste (and outcasts).
In the moist warmth
Everything was
Earnest and relaxed.

Next day was a little cooler
And I found the party leftovers –
A landscape of red,
A seething curry of mosquito bites
Strewn all over
The balcony of my body.

Ghosts

Daylight's husk
Falls away.

From the west
Squadrons of kites,
Ghosts of the dusk,
Fly – silent, staring down.
Where are they going?

On the waterway
Boats pass, winking red – green – red –
Like ghost boats. They carry
Huddles of passengers.
Where are they going?

I sit under a canopy roof
Like a ghost, drink beer,
And watch a man with an oxyacetelene blowtorch
Mend his car.

And when all's done,
Where will he go?

Three : A False Move

Madurai: A Dream

Woolgathering ...
We want to find
A bus, bike, bullock cart, car
To our Madurai of the mind.

The Myth of Madurai

"I will make my city the centre of the world."
Bold was the declaration of new-crowned Meenakshi, bold was her ambition,
For domination was her aim, and conquest her game.
She reposed on the flowerbed throne of the world (her world) facing west
So the sun rose behind her and the purple, yellow, pinking stripes of its power
Dazzled and dappled
Her admiring people,
And the hundred trunk-uplifted elephants, and the tens of caged alarming tigers, and the unknown unseen geckos slithering in the crevices of the walls of her citadel.

Meenakshi was beautiful.
Her eyes, large as fishes, were bright as the scales of the swimming fish in the clear waters of the Lakshadweep coral sea.
Her breasts rose like the mountains of the Cardamom Hills to the west – or, better, Mount Kailash, which she'd never seen.

Her movement, when she walked or turned was as graceful as *lasya*, the Tamil dance whose decorative designs and quick flowing patterns baffle the senses and entice the watcher's gaze.
Her lips were red as desire.

"I will make my city
The centre of the world,"
She breathed. She meant it. Behind the seductive presence, the graceful gestures with hand and arm, the slow reluctance of her enquiring face and turning head,
Meenakshi meant
What she said.

*   *   *   *

But Mount Kailash is the centre of the world.

Mount Kailash, where the sun warms the blood but cannot melt the ice;
Mount Kailash, where the snow sits light as dew, each crystal flake a diamond of light, no more;
Mount Kailash, where the idea of the world floats;
Mount Kailash, mother and father of all we can see, seed of life, source of the waters of life.

So Meenakshi had no alternative.
"It is my *dharma*," she muttered,
And a thousand butterflies fluttered into sunlight from the shade of the flowering fruit trees.
"I will go to Mount Kailash.
I will take my armies
And claim my desire."

*   *   *   *

The wheels of the carts squealed, the bullocks sweated, the great machines of war were hauled through the sweltering valleys of central India.

The soldiers marched barefoot, their steel weapons so hot they must wear gloves to hold them,
And the gloves made their hands sweat.

Meenakshi was borne in her *vahanna** by four giants
Whose heat sufferings were marks of honour.
"It is my *dharma*," she told herself, and she fanned her temples and clung to the shade.
Their *dharma* was harder.

And through the plains of the Deccan, Meenakshi's armies defeated nizams and maharajahs and zamorins and siguidars.
Death, blood, devastation
Marked Meenakshi's assertion of power.
Screams
Marked her progress.

When her armies reached the Himalaya, the air cooled, and as they climbed upwards towards the roof of the world, upwards towards the north,
The cold bit them like mangy dogs.
The air thinned, the rocks were icy screes.
The pack animals strained and dropped, incapable of more sacrifice,
The warriors panted and snorted, put their heads down, grunted dissatisfaction, and yomped on.
And the rains and the sleet and the hail came, steely arrows of frozen water in bolls like bullets.
Then they reached the plain of Tibet.

Before them – Mount Kailash, rising gently to the clouds, disappearing into vapour.

The gods themselves descended and deployed their troops in battle order,
A mighty host.
Meenakshi's exhausted force
Faced them. A pause, when perhaps some prayed, perhaps
Some foresaw their own bloody demise.

Then the two armies came together like stags in the rut.
Locked in combat, the whole swaying mass pushed first back, then forward, and over the thrashing thousands steam rose, and hung poised like rainclouds,
As if in mockery of the sacred mountain itself.
Till, like a boat which hits a rock, the gods' army split, splintered and shattered,
And Meenakshi was victorious.

The gods themselves were defeated,
And Sundareshwara, leader of their battalions, stood as if naked before the triumphant, passionate, power-hungry queen.
He was still as a cormorant on a rock.
He was tall as a young coconut palm, and strong as coconut shell.
His skin shone with ayurvedic oils, and his hair, black, with waves like the sea, reflected the light like a curving mirror.
He wore nothing but a loin cloth and sandals on his feet, in spite of the cold.
And he stared out of eyes which were clear as glacier water.
Sundareshwara – worthy re-embodiment of Shiva the destroyer?

* * * *

Meenakshi faced Sundareshwara over a field strewn with corpses.
Over a battleground littered with the bodies of the dead, Sundareshwara faced Meenakshi.

And a thing stronger than death floated like a cloud between them.
Her eye, her brow, the neatness of her nose, the slow smiling of her lips, her little chin, her smooth youthful neck
Entranced him.
His hair, his jaw, his sideburns deep-coloured and curly, the cool charcoal of his eye, his teeth, his tongue just visible between his teeth

Excited her.
She stood still,
While he made towards her,
Bent his back in the obeisance of the meek.
She took his hand in hers.
He looked down, then up into her face.
Eyes meeting, they said – or perhaps thought –
"Yes."

Sundareshwara sighed.
Meenakshi gripped his hand. She was the victor. And she wanted to make Madurai
The centre of the world.
But this Sundareshwara –
He was something she hadn't bargained for.

While he sighed, and his grey eyes dilated,
Her brain fizzed with
What must be done,
And what must be done was
To load whatever was left, to direct whoever remained, and to order the march back to Madurai.

And the enchanting Sundareshwara –
He must come with her.

       *   *   *   *

The return to Madurai took forty-four days
And forty-four nights.
Sundareshwara was permitted to ride in Meenakshi's *vahanna*.
The bearers strained harder. Her orders were: "Carry the *vahanna* more smoothly
Than a snake slithering,
Than a boat sailing on a still lake,
Than a breath of wind on a spring afternoon,"
And the carriers sweated and struggled.

But when the palanquin jolted, even ever such a little,
Sundareshwara found his hand
Leaping to Meenakshi's cheek, her shoulder, even her breast,
And Meenakshi was forced to force him to desist.

At night when they'd camped and eaten what food the place could yield up,
They lay in the same tent,
But apart.
And Meenakshi ordered her servants: "Make the night velvet
That our sleep will be peaceful, our dreams light as the breast feathers of a night heron."
So they played the *nagaswaram*, the low-toned flute of Tamil Nadu, as gently as dawn breaks,
They made a fire by the tent entrance out of last year's fruit leaves, as soothing as the sky's stars,
They lit sandalwood incense sticks, as sweet as sugar plums.

Every evening Sundareshwara found a means to approach Meenakshi's bed,
And every evening Meenakshi shooed him away
Like a henwife with a cheeky chicken.

She refused his importunate advances.

* * * *

On the forty-fifth day they reached Madurai.

Meenakshi, the virgin queen, and her promised consort, Sundareshwara, were greeted by crowds of people with garlands of a thousand petals.
And there was dancing in the streets of the city
And music
And a parade of a hundred decorated elephants.

A huge square reservoir was dug outside the city walls
And the water of the River Vaigai was channelled into it by the diligence of subtle engineers.

A square island was built in the centre of the square reservoir
And a pink-walled, many-pinnacled square temple constructed in its centre.
And at the centre of that centre burned
The holy flame.

A boat with twelve hundred burning candles on its deck and twice that number of flower heads scattered across poop and bows
Floated slowly to the temple, bearing Meenakshi and Sundareshwara
To their wedding.
There was music, dancing, wild chanting and thick clouds of the strangest incense.
Sundareshwara placed the garland of flowerheads three times round Meenakshi's neck,
And she placed it three times round his.
They walked seven times clockwise round the sacred flame.
The priests knotted their two robes together.
The cymbals, the flutes, the drums pranced in the ears,
The true, the honoured rites were accomplished,
The priests bowed,
And the people huzzah'd,
Till it seemed all the plains of Tamil Nadu, and all the beasts and birds and reptiles and plants applauded, too.
For the lovers were united.

*   *   *   *

That night, at last, Sundareshwara, bathed and oiled and perfumed with the musk of desire,
Was lifted into his *vahanna* on the orders of the queen
And carried through the corridors of the palace that was a temple, with music braying and incense blowing,
Until at last
He came to Meenakshi.
Now they were truly united.

Lovemaking became lifemaking.

But then
The desert beetle of doubt burrowed into the chambers of her mind:
How to keep him hers? how to
Keep love true?

And in the most secret places of her brain, in the cellars of her mind, she slowly, slowly began
To chuckle with delight: she devised a scheme to test him.
She knew (and he knew) he had the weakness of men – a wandering eye, a certain whimsy, a brain sometimes idle.
So Meenakshi caused to be brought naked before him a beautiful virgin, with slim hips and high cheekbones and, of course, fish eyes.
And Sundareshwara was tempted.

The virgin's eyes fluttered downwards (Meenakshi her teacher).
Sundareshwara stirred.
In the pause of an aeon, a second, the world teetered, its walls trembled,
Till Sundareshwara turned away.
He was
Enthralled,
He was
In thrall
To Meenakshi.

From that day to this, every day, the reverent holy men who are also her servants have done what she commanded:
Even today, every day, they bear the willing Sundareshwara to her bed at evening,
Once each year she tempts him
But Sundareshwara resists, knowing that the beautiful Meenakshi's fertile imagination will provide the endless variety of delights which can never satiate.
For Meenashki embodies his *dharma*.

And every night she couples with him in endless passionate lovemaking.
The heat of their passion outburns even the pitiless south Indian sun!

But is Madurai the centre of the world?

Performing Madurai

The Elephant in the Temple

Like a slowly-moving sculpture
(One among thousands in Meenakshi's temple)
The heavy elephant waits. Face
Cutified in Shiva white – dashes and swirls –
He stands and ponders,
While his keeper,
Stage-manager with proud moustache,
Takes coins (or notes)
To make the old thing dance.
He repeats again
What's been rehearsed,
Gently upholding his curvy trunk
To be flash-snapped,
And breathing hot, moist air
Over a pinky cheek …
And then – that's all. The elephant
Has performed his part, his keeper's
Done what was required, and
Home goes the tourist,
Ten rupees lighter, but
Chuckling, perhaps.

Getting Married

The brahmins stand like actors in the wings
Awaiting their cue:
A nervous giggle, a glance around,
Deliberate composing of face and posture.
I offer a banknote. Immediately
A chubby fellow, brown belly
Over pure white loincloth,
Precious thread his special prop,
Pops up. A godly player,
He bows, palms together,
And skips and jogs
Into his holy sanctum. He hauls out
Ash, ochre, a flame sweet-scented
In a dull bronze holder.
My face is smeared, your forehead
Daubed. We put our hands
Into the flame, then touch
Our cheeks, eyelids, brows.
Water to wash,
Music to make
Our muse awake.
The performance climaxes:
The brahmin offers
Marigolds, a garland,
Green, and orange, and white: it's heavy
When he gently lowers it
Onto my shoulders. Then he signs
That I must remove and put it on
Your shoulders, then
You must do the same for me.
The ritual is enacted thrice.
Self-consciously, we smile, and
The brahmin also smiles,
Almost claps his hands,
But seems suddenly to remember
He too acts in this; so now
Pronounces us 'man and wife'

(But is this true?), then trots back
To his friends, leaving us –
United, reunited – both poorer,
And richer.

Purapattu : **Processing**

In the temple of the secret goddess,
Fish-eyed Meenakshi of the beautiful breasts,
We await the rite of love.
Bare feet whisper on the stone floorway,
The brahmins almost nervously
Fiddle with their sacred threads – this,
They know, is no mere performance.

At once, a shifting of eyes, feet,
An upbeat of the heart.
The deep-toned flute of reverence and desire,
The *nagaswaram*, blares, and torches,
Symbols of the burning *lingum**, flare.
Purapattu: the setting forth.

The people crane and grin for *darshan** –
To see the god – Shiva – Sundareshwara –
Borne along swan-stately
In his silver shell-like palanquin
By brahmins bare-chested, golden-earringed.

While cymbals clang and clash,
And *tavil* rolls, people push out,
Pull back, in smoky, incense-flavoured gloom.
Past pillars – thin shadows strangely posed –
And holy pictures – colours, patterns, shapes now weird –
The odd, ungainly crew –
Snake-shrewd music, shivering flames, and smoke –
Process, unsung secrets pulsing, pulsing.

At the entrance to Meenakshi's chamber,
They stop. The *vahanna* is set down,
But not for rest, not rest.
Incense swirls, richer, more enticing,
While the god's feet are washed, scented, adorned
(He is to tread the carpet of the beautiful),
And drums and low-tuned flute
Wail with yearning, desire
Almost unattainable, almost
Beyond our most fantastic fancies,
But real, and here and now.

The priests pass three times clockwise
Round the recumbent god.
At last, the moment.
The people step back, breathless,
The Brahmins grasp the silver poles: only they
May enter the boudoir of the goddess,
Her inner sanctum, transporting there
Priapic Shiva to his coupling.

And when it's morning,
Tomorrow's light, we know
This one night's jointure
Has been, will be
For ever and ever.

The Story of Madurai

Long long ago

The south – the roasting pan of India, the dust bath of al-Hind, the brilliant paint pot of the subcontinent.
Its people – Dravidians – dark skins, high cheekbones, lithe, graceful, beautiful.

Here was a legendary empire, built by the people under their leaders, the Pandyas.
They made Madurai an artwork of civilisation, and a rampart against northerners' angry ambition.

They built temples and palaces, yes, and small houses for the people. And they built *sangams* – academies for poets, which taught imagery and imagination, verse and the word. Eight thousand poets graduated from Madurai's *sangams*, and they created epic poems recounting the Dravidian myths, celebrating Dravidian ways and Dravidian life.

From these poets' words were born dance, the dance of the gracious temple women now frozen in sculpture; and music, the music you can still hear in the shawm, the barrel drum and the sweet wailing songs of south India.

This was the glory of Madurai before Madurai, a mythical city, floating on the lake of legend.

And then ...

Centuries passed like the twittering of parakeets.
Today, far to the north, there's a village of old bricks, tumbled rubble, and brushwood growing between stones. Was it the hills here, or the macaques, or the disputations of religion, which made this place
Imperial? The empire of the Vijayanagars.
And as empires, like cacti, must grow, so the Vijayanagars' outshoots, its outgrowths and outpourings, took its wealth and its life scrolls out through the southern plains
To Madurai.
Vijayanagar's silk markets, palaces, spice recipes, toys gave a new ebullience to Madurai.
Its bazaars, its roses, fragrant as pillow talk, its peacocks with eyes in their tails, its cut blue emeralds, its works of art, paintings, sculptures, hand-made embroideries, infiltrated Madurai's heart.

But the Vijayanagar empire was too vast. It needed administrators.
Administrators! The word betrays itself: 'imperial administrators' contracts to 'traitors'.
The Nayaks – the emperor's chosen surrogates – stole power for themselves and
A new Madurai bloomed,
Their Madurai:
A city laid out like a lotus, whose petals co-exist in equality;
A city laid out like a mandala, for the people to walk in, threading their own mystic truths;
A city centred on its temple.

This was Madurai the beautiful,
Madurai the ravishing, the mystical, the sandalwood smoke among cities.

And now ...

Madurai betrayed.
The poets have sung their songs. Now they are silent.
The dancers have danced, and scuttled into the wings, their only echo – the ungainly rush of pedestrians fleeing the blaring traffic, passing their days amid rubbish piles and exhaust fumes.

The lotus is begrimed, its petals wilted.
The mandala is smeared with the long streams of neglect.

No longer do the rulers care for the aspirations of the temple, the means of its heart music.
No longer do they desire to be
The centre of the world.
Today's rulers* are film stars, cutthroats, pirates of culture,
Bathed in the acid of self-importance.

And all that's left of Madurai is
The performance of Madurai.

Madurai: a Reality

Madurai Temple towers covered in coconut leaves.

When we reached Madurai – hours on winding, barely-tarmaced roads, with horns blaring, corners blindly rushed, through litter-angry streets and urine-stinking air –
The gods, the carvings had retreated. They were
Invisible. Was it our bad tempers, impatience with the mess, the filth, the smashing, migraine-making, have-no-patience racket
That made the object of our journey
Withdraw? Can we know a reason?
The temple towers were all covered in builders' screens.
Dry coconut leaves*, rotting, made
Dull pepperpot pinnacles without faces, poking listlessly at clouds.
Where was
The Madurai of dreams?

Four : The Song of South India

A New Start

Rushing blindly to Madurai
Used neither head nor heart;
There's no regeneration that way –
Time for a fresh start.

What can south India really give?
Should we think or feel?
Here's where the journey really starts,
Here's where things get real.

The Cricket and the Bony Cow

Six a.m.
And a cricket under my window
Is rasping at the darkness
While I
Am dreaming of a bony cow,
Horns painted
Orange and blue.

Light begins to leak.
The cricket goes on
Scraping away
While I
Forget the bony cow,
Dream of something
Entirely new.

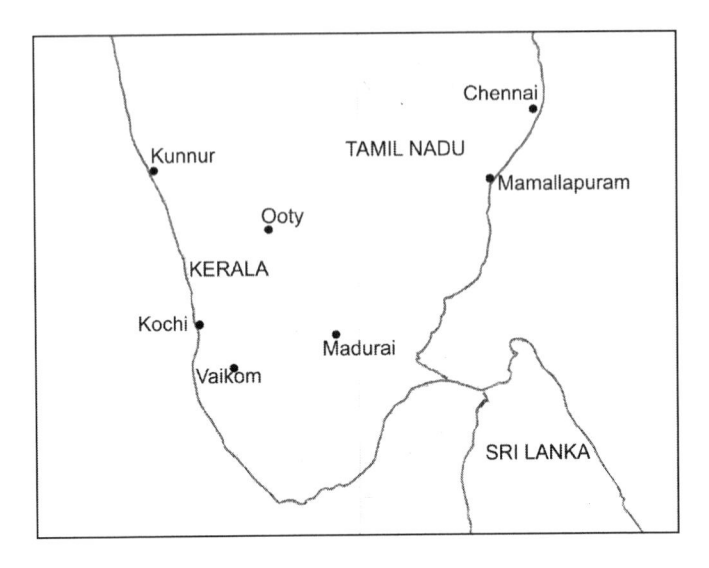

South India

Yes – we need to find a different place – breathe
Fresh air. Restless as ants, we turn and seek and search, reach
Green-leafed, sun-sprung Mamallapuram. Maybe this ancient
    place
Has something to teach.

Rain in Mamallapuram

The sad rain rains on the street:
Thatched roofs sag,
Red earth churns,
Turns to mud.

But still –
This world's astir:
Pink ribbons streaming, a barefoot child
Treads dainty
Through a wide, rust-brown puddle;
A fierce-faced aunt steps out
Fiercely – but
Her umbrella spokes
Are bent, half-broken,
Her spangled sari's sopping;
And a lad,
Dwarfed by his gigantic shopping-bag,
Grins, skip-splashes in the gutter,
Admires himself in a parked car mirror,
Swaggers on, damply, shop-wards.

The eaves drip,
Puddles ping and hop with drops,
And the sad rain
Rains and rains.
But people here
Step lively.

The Necklace

Our feet feel their way
Over ruts and scars
On the rain-ruined road,
Find themselves outside
The stone souvenir maker's stall.
My eye catches
A little snake
Or lizard, deftly shaped
By artist unknown,
Brown, and seeming to crawl,
Smooth belly over unresponsive earth.
The man threads it on a lace

And I buy it for you.
Our eyes meet.

That night, listening to the rain, we
Tiptoe into the way of the wind,
And poetry slow-waltzes in the shadows.

And when the sweaty sun
Has wafted the wet away,
Again we stand outside
The carved memory seller's stall.
And this time
You buy me
A tiny Shiva *lingum*
No bigger than my fingernail.
Black, shiny, the image
Enters the *yoni**
Proudly: it's struck from stone.
This too is threaded on a lace,
And when we walk away together,
I'm wearing it round my neck
Proudly.

Secrets in Stone*

Krishna*

I met a rickshaw driver on the road
Who said: I'll show you
All the ancient carved stone mysteries
Of Mamallapuram – reclining Vishnu*,

The Bhima *ratha**, the temple on the shore
Where every sculpted human limb, bull's ear
And towering pinnacle's planed
By sea winds of a thousand years;

And Krishna, shielding folk from cyclone's fury,
Holding up a mountain; making music with his flute
So pure it can't be carved; and milking cows,
Pails of rich, nutritious cream, enough
To make a vast delicious butter-ball –
A boulder where today the tourists pose.

Krishna's butter ball, Mamallapuram

Durga*

I met a man in sandals and striped shirt
Who said: I'll show you
The tide of turbulent humanity, battle-tossed,
Falling, standing, crouching, straight, askew.

Eight-armed Durga (also Kali)
Rides astride a lion, bow in hand,
Topples club-flailing Mahisha*,
While her attendants greet his end.

She dances his death – stands in the stirrups,
Sways back and forward, bow outflung,
Back for the quivered arrow,
Forward to load, draw back the bowstring,
Shoot – the forward leap, following the dart –
Poetry of movement become petrific art.

Arjuna*

I met an old man hawking postcards
Who said: I'll show you
The teeming world set in a single rock:
Look – hunters, wise men, kings and beggars, too.

Here elephants stand huge, their doubtful young
Small under their bellies; there, lion and deer
Rest together; beyond, a cat considers …
Beside cascading Ganga, none feels fear.

One figure's out of kilter with the rest –
Arjuna. In an agony of penance, on one leg
He stands … endures. The rhythm of life
Is not his rhythm. His self-scourging begs
The question: Will this obtain relief?
And we? Can we reach Kailash scarred with grief?

Arjuna's Penance : Arjuna is seen standing on one leg on the left hand side near the top.

Going On

Midnight. I sit, cramped, awkward, at a wonky hotel table,
    pondering:
Sense sculpted in stone?
Self-certified,
Blood, brain, bone?

Am I telling true?
Will scribbling this stuff
Help on the journey? Is it
Enough?

Stone cedes
To high street, high road:
The way of the journey
Justifies the load.

On the Road

We are exhorted:

Sound horn
Careful drive. Get home alive
Danger lurking at blind corners
Say No to mobile while U R mobile
Impatient on road. Patient in hospital
Your loving family is waiting for you at home
Hurry causes worry

These maxims please us
Even while they tease us.
Clichés – yes,
But containing some pebbles of truth, nonetheless.

Level Crossing

The gate guillotines
Raucous hordes.

Silence settles.

Somewhere someone coughs.
Two fields away a goat bleats.
The dust drops.

Then the train hoots, rattles by, and
The hell-for-leathering starts
All over again.

And Yet the Sea

Hearing its booming whisper
We came to the vast sea
Down a narrow littery way.

Grey, grey, its tracery of repeating waves
Reaching, reaching, then pouring forward,
Breaker upon breaker,
Breakers upon breakers,
And small wave-ends
Squirming and curling at our feet.
And the sighing and the panting
Of the surge upon surge
Purged us, urged us
To something, something ...

We turned, wind-wetted,
Walked on perfect pancake sands,
Heads high, while our feet
Dodged litter piles, shit lumps,
Empty cardboard cups, cellophane

Fluttering and tumbling,
Then stalled:
         a dead dog,
Plump as a cushion,
Four stiff stumps
Sticking out – frozen tongues
Insulting us. Appalled,
We retreated,
Hearts beating, foreheads
Crazy-paved with wrinkles.

And yet the sea …

Still Travelling

We journey
Through ways too various to tell,
Round hairpin bends, past toddy shops, spice gardens,
    through dusty hill villages,
And stop at some convenient hotel.

Vijay

Hot days, cold nights.
After dinner, the bell croaks.
It's Vijay. He produces
Laundry, clean towels, extra blankets,
And, from his pockets,
Soap, shampoo, toilet rolls. He grins.
A latter-day Robert Houdin,*
He knows all about style.

He is tall, loose-limbed,
And white, irregular teeth lilt
When he laughs.

'Where you from, sir?
Ah, Scotland' – as if he were
South India's Bartholomew.*

He lays a bundle of sticks
Criss-cross in the fireplace,
Slops on drops of kerosene,
And, Promethean,
Sets it ablaze.
'Have a good night, sir.'
And he's off into the dark,
Leaving us warm
Within as well as without.

Theyyam*

Performance at Kerala Kathakali Centre

Drum drums dumb the brain,
Pain-beat the pulse,
Conjure
Ten-foot-tall god-man:
Snake-painted body,
Broad board lips, pompoms, tassels jigging
On towering crown head –
Unreal reality plain before us.

His stamping, twirling, beating
Knocks thinking to humdrum ...
Stops,
Stares

Till you flinch,
Are swallowed by
Earthquaking tectonic platters,

Howling ankles, feathering and brandishing
Brain pain … again again …

Outside –
Pelting rain
Slams the windscreen, bounces
Like a billion ping pong balls
Off car bonnet, roadway …
For a moment clouds are
Pink sheets, billowing –
Then black again, blind.
The thunder snarls.

We lie in our beds.
We know it's show.
We are
Mute against angry gods.

Kali

Kali, ancient goddess, egg of the earth, mother of all,
Kali, goddess of fire, water, stone,
Black goddess, white goddess,
Kali, whose green face is the forests and grasslands,
Whose brown breasts are the earth, the soil, the rock,
Kali, who comes before all, and whose spirit makes
Streams flow, wood burn, stones stand,
Cares for all of us.

But Daria* was jealous – no-one cared for him.
So he turned three times about, and made smallpox.
He coated the worm of smallpox in sugar
And he offered it to the people.
– Sweet on the tongue, dissolves in a moment, leaves you
     feeling
Different.

The people
Swallowed Daria's story,
Swallowed smallpox,
And fell into fever.
Red, bursting, stabbing fever.
And their smooth skin burst and bled and scabbed.

They ran to Kali, mother goddess.
– We are your people.
But see how you care for us.
We burn, we boil with fever,
And all over our bodies
Scabs of badness
Sprout through our skin.

Kali looked, and her heart beat.
She uncoiled her long red tongue,
Long as a snake, red as evening sun,
And she licked the skin of her people.
With her long red tongue,
Kali licked off every scab of smallpox
From the skin of her people.

Then she went to Daria.
Daria was holding a chicken in his hands –
A protection charm.
White feathers dithering,
Eye round as a target,
Legs scaley yellow.
It saw Kali coming.
It flapped urgently.
Daria tightened his grip,
Held the chicken out
Towards Kali, almost
Meek, almost like
Obeisance.

Kali took the chicken's neck,
And one swift twist

Broke it.
The chicken's head
Flopped over,
Its wings
Dropped.

And Daria was dead.

Muttupan

Once there was a woman called Kalakot Nambudiri.
She worked hard in the fields, but she didn't sleep well, she was one of the outcasts of the village.
She worked hard, but she was still poor.
And she wanted a child.
She prayed to Lord Shiva, and Lord Shiva heard her.
He appeared before her, took her in his arms and gently lay with her.
She conceived a boy child, whom she named Muttupan.

Young Muttupan grew quickly
But as he grew, so naughtiness grew with him:
Instead of respecting all life (as a good Hindu should), he fashioned for himself a small bow, sharp slender arrows,
And he stood on the bank of the river, watching.
Soon a silver fish scooted and turned. A slender arrow flew sizzing through the air. Muttupan laughed, and pulled the fish, its silvery scales, out of the water.
Then he made a fire, and cooked and ate the fish.

A little time, and a little time, and Muttupan, this naughty boy, learned a new trick. Eat what is forbidden, drink what is forbidden.
He tapped the bark of the coconut palm, he dropped the drips into his pot and out of the juice of the palm tree he made
Something surprisingly delicious, something surprisingly exciting.

And after he'd drunk it, he tumbled into a deep steep sleep.

His mother didn't know what to do with him.
She worked every day in the field.
She couldn't care for him, nor could she control him, his doings.
So she hired him out as a labourer to a distant bigwig, a Brahmin of high reputation.
The Brahmin set Muttupan to watching his herd of long-horned holy cattle, and warned him not to let any tigers approach.
If he saw a tiger nearby, the boy was to bang with a ladle on the large tin bowl which the Brahmin gave him for the purpose.
That would frighten tigers away.

Muttupan watched the holy cattle grazing peacefully. No tigers came near. Muttupan became bored.
Into the large tin bowl, he dripped the sap of the coconut palms, added water, and soon he had brewed up his special something strong and delicious to drink.
Then he noticed the melon-like dillyband of one of the holy cows he was guarding.
Approaching the cow, he placed the tin bowl with the strong drink under its holy dillyband, pulled the little holy danders hanging down from the dillyband, and drew off cool creamy milk.
It splashed into the bowl, mixed with Muttupan's potent preparation, and made toddy.
Muttupan, laughing, drank it. This was better even than the first delicious, exciting drink he'd brewed. And there was plenty of it.
Pretty soon he was lying under a tree, deep asleep and smiling happily.

No tigers came while he slept.
But the Brahmin of high reputation came.
He saw Muttupan sleeping.
He was horrified.

Muttupan would probably have had a scare,
Even if the Brahmin of high reputation hadn't beaten him.
But the Brahmin did beat him,
And gave Muttupan a very sore head.

But Muttupan discovered that he had more than just one soreness in his head: he found his thinking was making another soreness slap on top of the first one. Soreness upon soreness.
What was he to do now?
Where was he to go?
Away he wandered, leaving the Brahmin alone with his high reputation and his holy cows.

And the women working in the fields noticed this wanderer, lonely as a mongoose, handsome as a hawk. Out cast.
They made up to him. Who was he?
He offered them fish and gave them something surprisingly delicious, surprisingly exciting to drink.
He made them smile
And feel more wanted than ever they did in the fields, than ever they did in the village.
And he gave them the blessing of sleep at night.
They wondered who he was.
Perhaps the spirit of Kali, mother goddess, who fed them, and watched them when they went to bed?

So it was that Muttupan, though he was a son of Lord Shiva, yet became the spirit of Kali.
And he was worshipped by the poor people, those who worked all day in sun-heavy fields, and yet who were excluded from the fruits of their work.
They made him the god of their outcast state, and performed his ritual,
When his spirit, the spirit of Kali, entered the person of the priest, and eased for a little their lives –
Not least with his gifts of fish and toddy.

The ritual became known as Theyyam.

Performance in a north Keralan village

I am an outsider
Watching a young man
In a dark hut (not
An official temple,
Not a temple)
Daub his body with paint.
The paint is rice paste, turmeric,
And charcoal salved with oil.
Time passes slowly.
Slowly he becomes
Decorative, unworldly.

Prasaad – gifts.
A man with bald head,
Check shirt,
Offers
Me and everyone
Slivers of boiled fish
With rice, on a banana leaf,
And a surprisingly delicious
Warm, brown drink.
First to one guest, then the next,
Then the next. Each guest
Gets due attention.

The young man's body
Flaunts tiger stripes.
Anklets jangling, skirt scarlet,
And cheeks wide-pouched,
He stands a moment,
And in a moment
Dons the high headdress.
Even I see
How he is transformed.
The god enters his body
Like a long snake
Sliding into a hide.

Theyyam performance in a village near Kunnur, Kerala.

Then comes the frenzy –
Drums and cymbals, weird wild *kuzhal*
Calling, aching, forlorn in the dusk,
Priest stamping, dancing,
God swaying like a rich red reed
In whirling wind.
I feel my own breath come shorter,
And my eyes wet.
The priest pours oil on the altar,

Lays on banana leaves, flowers,
Pours oil again, again banana leaves,
And always waves the flaming lamps
Round and around the offering.
Music swirls, the god
Stabs with his spear
The sacred coconut.
The milk ejaculates.

Is he possessed? Could he
Enter the flame and remain
Unscalded? Slash himself
And stay unwounded?
I crane and stare
And his stately skip
And lowering glare
Declare
Nothing.

Is this
The angry god?
He? – whom the people now crowd round,
Flock to, seek help from, succour, blessing?

Stone, fire, water
And the strange music of the not-world
Light the paradox of not-magic.
The people believe, accept, rejoice,
And I, an outsider,
Hear the silence in their voice.

By the Way

The way to Mount Kailash
Is not easy to find.
Airport, road, railway are all very well, but
This is also a journey of the mind.

King Cobra

I saw king cobra once,
Wheat brown and black, hooded, huge,
In the burning heat of southern India.

Having some regal business, I suppose,
On the far verge of the road,
He began to slither
Over the scalding tarmac.
But, belly burning, he turned – too late –
And writhed, maddened,
Out of his kingdom. And a bearded lorry man
Leapt from his cab, grabbed stones
And hurled them. The second
Broke the cobra's back, the fourth
Fell full on the skull,
Dashed it to death.

The lorry driver,
Reckless and dainty,
Scooped up the loops
Of twisting scales, dumped them
In the ditch, drove on.
And so did we,
Commoners in the interfering world.

Mongoose

In the clearing of dead leaves,
Dry sticks, where I sat, daydreamed,
Something emerged, alive, inquisitive –
Mongoose.
Silent as sun and shadow, secure
In furry camouflage,
It stopped, head a-tilt,
Sensing a presence, and glanced back
Over its shoulder
At me. Disdainful, perhaps,
Or busy, it looked away, moved on
A step or two, then
Looked again. And I looked back
While pale time paused.
A bird scuffled, crickets whirred,
Maybe a yellow leaf drifted
Down the feathery air,
When the mongoose and I
Eyed one another, almost companions.
Then he pushed on into the undergrowth,
Insouciant, contented,
And I remained
Listening to crickets.

Elephant Festival*

All Roads

All day we waited, like dry earth for rain,
    And all day the tension grumbled;
All day the roads were walked by the people,
    All pushing on to the Temple.

All day the roads were for walkers only,
    The battalions of Shiva's army –
Fresh faces, beards, bare feet, chappals,
    Women in silk bright saris.

Here a dark woman giggles with her friend,
    Gives her a friendly stare,
Then ties a sun-riped orange-yellow flower-burst
    In her long black shining hair.

There a policeman, lighthouse-stern,
    Stands firm in the people-storm;
But he unbends to answer the pretty questions
    Of the prettiest girls in the swarm.

The streets are lined with bright-lighted stalls,
    Beseeching, begging rupees:
7-Up, cashew nuts, hand stamps, toys,
    At least a penny whistle – please!

A shaky, hand-cranked, ancient mangle
    Shreds yellow fibre strips,
Squeezes out the essence of sugar cane soda,
    Sweetest sweetness for thirsty lips.

In a darkened hut under the temple walls
    We leave our shoes with the hairy man,
And move with the crowd through the high-arched gate,
    And the higgledy-piggledy hurly-burly's gone.

In the Temple

In the Temple, people follow the sign
Towards the elemental shrine.
They touch their foreheads, genuflect,
And give the god his due respect.

To please him, too, in other ways,
Music in the courtyard plays.
Eager crowds sit still and mute
Before the endless drums and flute,
But though they might be almost numb,
They're readying themselves for what's to come.

In a distant corner on the sand,
A slow grey elephant lonely stands,
Swaying and watching with tiny eyes.
Perhaps he's here to symbolise
– As dusk reduces afternoon –
The main event, what's coming soon.
Slowly people are coming alive:
Soon the elephants will arrive.

Rangoli: Vaikom Elephant Festival

Night Falls

This is the arch, brilliantly lit,
Set up where the elephants stand.

Now is the time to see god's face,
Painted in powder by artist's hand
Under the arch, brilliantly lit,
Set up where the elephants stand.

People crowd round, curiosity fanned,
To see god's face
Painted in powder by artist's hand
Under the arch, brilliantly lit,
Set up where the elephants stand.

Drums and cymbals form the band
To play for those whose curiosity's fanned
To see god's face
Painted in powder by artist's hand
Under the arch, brilliantly lit,
Set up where the elephants stand.

Priests light the lamps and flaming brands
Where drums and cymbals form the band
To play for those whose curiosity's fanned
To see god's face
Painted in powder by artist's hand
Under the arch, brilliantly lit,
Set up where the elephants stand.

Everything's ready, everything's planned
When priests light the lamps and flaming brands
Where drums and cymbals form the band
To play for those whose curiosity's fanned
To see god's face
Painted in powder by artist's hand
Under the arch, brilliantly lit,
Set up where the elephants stand.

The Elephants

Night. Near midnight.
Crowds thicker than ant swarms
Wait, breathe, expect.
A world on tiptoe.
Darkness
Holds its breath.
Shapes loom, huge in the dimness
– Elephants
Swaying like shadows,
Or shadows of shadows.
Foreheads gold-decked,
Headdresses mahout-high,
They stand sentry
To the entrance of the god.
Their ears flap,
Their trunks wrap
Round the felt presence.
In face of its essence,
Their eyes wink,
And in the blink of an eye
Their mystery plays over
The history of every day –
Prancing fire-circles dazzle, spray,
Nagaswarams shriek and bray,
Oil lamps flare and drip and spout,
Human voices shudder, shout,
Smoky incense swirls about –
Drums batter the night,
Screams, dreams ignite,
The elephants' monstrous height
Towers upwards, beyond sight, beyond
Flame frenzy, heart alight,
In the bite of now, how
Earth, noise, smoke, fire

Give birth, and life
Bursts out, sprouts,
Flouting fireworks,
Night become light.

Elephants, fire, a brilliantly lit arch, crowds of people.

What the South Sang

1

There is time to understand time
There is a time to understand
A time, any time, that time
The granite rock
Rolled into the long lagoon of the centuries
Smooth as a snake

There is time to understand how time understands
A time to be with time
With this second, and this, and this
In perpetual stasis
Perpetually in motion
Like the series of stills
In the moving picture

There is time to understand
The necessity to understand
The seconds which don't make up eternity
Time to understand
The longevity in the second
The stopping of the clock
Which allows time space
The before time the after time
The time between times

This is the time to understand
The past in the present
Time to be in the present
Balancing precariously
On the shoulders of the old ones
Those present in their time

There is time to understand
Time the riddling joker, saucy sorcerer
Conundrum incarnate, light inchoate
Time which allows the grass to be bowed and bent and beaten
    down
By the grey rains, the strong rains, arrows of water
And to stand taller
In consequence

Time
Fragments of discontent
Fragments of hope

2
Stone magus elephant

Pod of being
Petal of doing

Stone – foundation
Magus – performer
Elephant – anima

I breathe

I act
I do
I perform

I act the performance
I perform the action
I flower

I rehearse
I improvise

And there is only action in time
Only performance in the now
Only doing the action
To grow the petal
To make the performance

I act
I do
I perform

I am truth
I perform truth
Truth is
In the pod
In the petal
In the performing growth

In the soil
In the wind

Stone magus elephant

The flower
Does not rehearse
The flower
Does not learn
Its moves
The flower
Is in the pod
It acts
Flowering

    * * * *

This is the song of the south,
The song Mother India sang,
Time and times before the knell
For the European onslaught rang.

Time to move north.

Five : Still Life

The Rivers of the World

From Kailash, centre of the world's mandala, flow
The rivers of the world –

Brahmaputra, gurgling water,
Spilling, serpenting across Tibet,
Cascading, free-lading, snow-smudged
Through black gorge, green pass
To Assam, to Bangladesh,
Vast leviathon of water, writhing
To the mangrove delta of the Sunderbans;

Karnali, turquoise one,
Cutting through Himalaya, tumbling
And speeding, banks feeding
Elephants, sloth bears, blue bulls, depths
Hiding muggers and spike-toothed gharials,
Till India, when Karnali becomes
One with holy Ganga;

Indus, called 'lion river',
Civilizing far and further
Into the backwash of time;
Sundering subcontinent
From north and west, from peoples
Whose always ambition
Leads to the lands of the Harappans;*

And Kailash's fourth river –
China's Yellow River,
Hwang Ho, quickening the east –

Or so some say; but others
That it's Sutlej, the fourth falling water,
Joining Indus, seeking, searching, finding
The blue, free sea.*

   * * * *

Mount Kailash calls. We must answer.
Our fate – our *dharma* – hangs
Where we go – up the gurgling waters of the world to the
  holy mountain,
To get some end to the wrack of things.

So, gathering up
The pods, the petals of the south,
We head northwards, towards Kailash,
Aiming to follow the holy river there from its mouth.

Majestic, destructive Brahmaputra of Bengal
Begins at Sunderbans, where time seems to stall.
The water laps as it has always lapped,
But this place, changing with every turning tide, cannot be
  mapped.

Sunderbans

Still Life

 1
Still life: mud cottages, dry weeping thatch,
And three or four people
  Sitting, staring.

Our little craft chugs, chunters up the steel-green waters,
The channels, openings, streams
  Of India's lace collar.

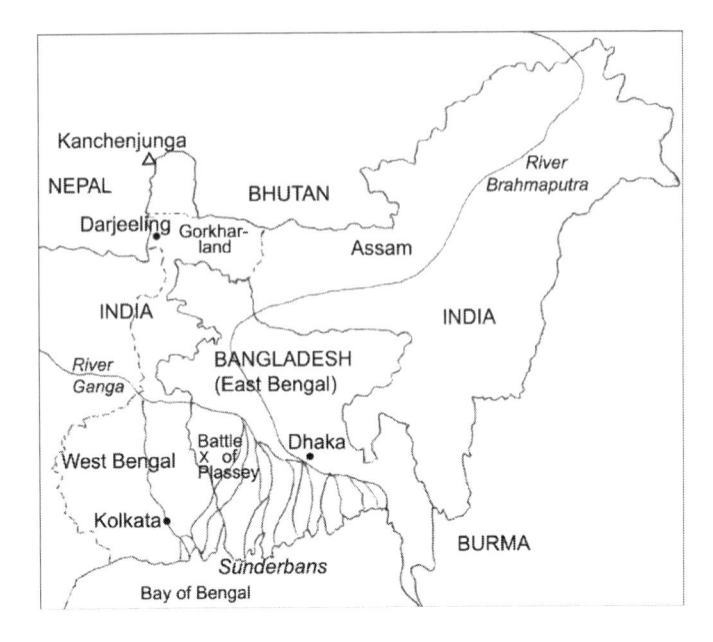

West and East Bengal

An osprey sits, waits. A giant lizard flops like a blot
In grey stalky grass. Mud slippers
    Flip and squirm.

A world to itself slides by: mudbanks under mangrove trees;
Black tree roots, slippery and shining;
    Sibilant softness lapping.

Beside a black, empty, bow-shaped boat, dry-beached,
A child stands on one leg, shades his eyes
    To watch us pass,

And the pinking evening drifts towards dark.
Everything seems painted, stilled;
    Yet all stirs.

2
It's morning, it's fog: a dense quiet, straining to see:
Who are we? The only answer a screech of parakeets
    Somewhere above;

Then stealth, silence, stillness.
Ghost-grey tree stumps, hag-shaped;
    An indecipherable ripple ...

Our driver starts the engine – a slow, low thrumming.
Then stops. No progress possible,
    Though the shadow of a bank floats.

The heaviness clings and lingers. Our hair is damp.
And when we peer out – trees dripping into mud,
    Mud dripped on by trees.

Sunderbans

You can hear the water lilting
Against the low banks; you can smell
    Gentle, invisible rot.

In the fog through which we all must steer,
The sun peers, a pale orange leaf:
    Life still.

Where Now?

Which way? Brahmaputra's Bangladesh. We're in India.
We cannot even start
Up the great river.
India and Bangladesh are separate, apart.
Why?

Bande Mataram!
  (*Sushil Sen remembers*)

I'm an old man now.
Wisps of whiskers get in my mouth
And tickle my nose,
And my belly rumbles disgustingly.
But then I was young,
And what a time to be young
And to live in Bengal.
Yes, there was hatred, wrong, injustice
And British soldiers with guns every other yard on
    Chowringhee*,
But we had life, we had comrades, and songs –
The words of Bankim Chandra Chatterjee* –

Bande Mataram!
Pray for the mother, eh?
Mother Bengal, Mother Kali*,
Mother of us all.

Yes, I could sing it, shout it out loud, even today!
And we could do with it today.
Better than snuffling into my damned moustache
Which won't lie still.
That's the trouble with breathing.

Bankim Chandra Chatterjee –
If ever there was poetry in a name,
Sure, that was it!
My name, now – Sushil Sen –
No lyricism in that, no romance –
Silly little name. Well …

Bankim Chandra Chatterjee was the first I came across
Who told us –
Spit out the British.
Rescue Kali, Bengal mother,
From these pink devils,
Even if it means,
Telling the beads of your life.
Yes.
Aurobindo Ghosh - he was another:
Kali is wrapped in cotton wool, he said,
Hidden away, gagged, suffocating.
She must be set free so she can
Swoop down
And set us free.
And you must swoop, too.

I couldn't swoop now. No swooping for me,
Now. But then …
Set us free! *Bande Mataram*!
And who are we? The people of Bengal.
All the people of Bengal.

I bang this old stick on the floor
Till my knuckles shiver and jar.
We are Bengalis, whatever our religion.
Take this, for instance:
For us, for all of us, in Bengal
Divali is not Divali, it's Kali *puja*.
In Ashan – say, October –
When there's no moon, at midnight –
Then we celebrate
Our Kali –
Candles, fireworks, feasting, singing,
And the sacrificing of black goats –
Black for Kali,
Black for midnight,
Black for the flags we flourished
When Bengal was sliced in two.

Yes ... but ... well, getting ahead of myself.
'One thing at a time, grandad' –
That's what my daughter – granddaughter – says.
And – 'Tell your story in the right order.' Yes.
Calcutta in those days – beginning of the century –
We were getting uppity – all of us, Moslems, Hindus, all of
    us.
Bengal for the Bengalis, eh? *All* Bengalis.
So Curzon* – Lord Curzon – Eton, Oxford, the British Tory
    party –
He spotted what was going on –
And 'Calcutta, Calcutta, I'll cut ′ er' –
That's what he said – 'Cut her down to size.
How? Build up Dhaka – Moslem majority –
Counter balance – like a pair of scales –
Make Dhaka heavier,
Calcutta'll float up, lose its feet on the ground,
Lose its edge.
Split Bengal in two.
Yes, yes, makes me chuckle, it's so obvious.
What do they say?
Divide and rule.

Yes.
Divide and rule.
Make Bengal two.
One part Hindu – the west, Calcutta –
One part Moslem – the east, Dhaka.
Then set the one
Against the other.'
So much for Curzon.
No – not so much. There was more. Much more.

Nineteenth of June 1904 it was.
I'll never forget that date, that day.
Partition.
The British laughed
While all Bengalis shrank:
We were shamed, fooled,
Divided
And ruled.

Oh, there were meetings, protests, petitions –
I remember Jyotindra Mohan Tagore* – 'Boycott British
    goods!'
I remember the crowds on the Maidan.
Crowds? More than crowds – people
As far as you could see – and further –
And all in one voice, deep as oceans –
'United Bengal!' 'No partition!'
'*Bande Mataram*!'
Yellow turbans we wore, all of us,
All of us, from east, from west,
And the black flags we flourished,
Black for Kali.

Curzon, of course – he knew best:
'Just a tiny minority …
Politically ambitious …
Irrelevant.'
He should know, someone said.
But he'd forgotten –

Asia was changing, Asia was moving on
And up.
Remember Japan,
And the casting down of Russia.
Asia could be
Europe's equal,
Europe's better.
But Lord Curzon –
He knew better,
He knew best.

The day of Partition, when Bengal was sliced in two,
No food was cooked, the pots stayed empty, the fires unlit;
Shops were closed, padlocks locked, stallholders all in
   mourning.
Even before dawn, the banks of the Hoogly were forested
   with people,
The ghats a-buzz – so many of us paraded, barefoot,
To wash in the purifying waters of the river,
While the prophet – prophet we realized then –
Rabindranath Tagore – led us in singing –
Banglar mati Banglar jal* –
His song, composed out of our sadness, our grief.

Pah! It leaves a bitter taste,
A taste of unripe lime, or fenugreek – ach, I spit it out.

British soldiers stood at every corner,
Groups of them galloped through the streets,
Even their horses snarling.
Us? We threw stones at them,
Dodged down Calcutta's alleyways,
Threw more stones,
Strung tripwires,
Built barricades.
And we fought them.
But what can bare hands, cotton shifts, chappals do
Against rifles, armour, horses, jackboots?
Sometimes we burned British goods –

Orange bonfires lighting up the night sky.

Our messages were written in Bengali,
Published in our paper – the 'Bande Mataram'.
And two summers after partition – no, three, I think –
We were still fighting –
Well, some of us were still fighting.
Curzon's lickspittles raided the paper,
Banned it, arrested those who worked on it,
Took them to court.
I was there.
We crowded out their precious courtroom,
Shouted, sang – *'Bande Mataram!'*
Till the British screamed in panic.
I can see the bluecoat's eyes – wide, staring in fear,
His eyebrows riding up his face
Like a horse leaping a gate ...
Yes – and he took me – me! – seized me,
Twisted my arm, nearly broke it,
And he held me down while his mate
Whipped me, fifteen strokes of the lash,
As the magistrate ordered
Out of his purple mouth.
'He was shouting
Those damned words!'

Yes. Have you ever been lashed? It hurts.
I just let him do it,
I didn't fight back,
And after each lash I let him know
Bengal was my mother,
Each time I spoke what he called
'Those damned words':
Bande Materam!
I spoke them strong and clear

Every time the lash fell:
Bande Mataram!
I can scarcely say it now

Without getting a lot of spittle on my whiskers.
But still I believe it – yes:
Bande Mataram!
Yes –
Bande Mataram!

Wait while I wipe my beard.

Cause the next year – at Kali *puja* –
When the sky and the earth were darkest –
I heard one of our friends –
I'll not tell the name, not even now –
Tempt us:
'This year, Kali demands a new sacrifice –
White goats,
Not black.'
Two bombs – two lives –
Two white British goats.

That's enough.
I'm an old man, I can't go on chattering.
But see today –
East Bengal, Bangladesh.
And how many lives has that cost?
Curzon isn't here to see it, but think –
At Partition, not Independence,
And then again when East Bengal split off
From the west, the Punjab and Sind and …
Pah! I need my *chai*
And some *chana sattu**.
I can hold that down,
And my belly keeps quiet
After *chana sattu*.
And I'd like a cloth
To wipe the dribble off my beard.

That's all.
But if ever you hear the cry –
Bande Mataram!

Think of Sushil Sen.
Not this old codger
But a young fellow in a yellow turban,
Full of hope, full of life,
Singing with his comrades,
Calling Bengalis in the name of Bengal's mother.
Think of his whipping,
And the whipping of Bengal.
And how we knew,
What we knew …

And then think –
And I spit again –
What Curzon knew –
All he knew was
That he knew best.

*   *   *   *

So Bengal was ripped in two,
And now travellers to India cannot go where the Brahmaputra
    goes.
Self-doubting, with trepidation, we follow a path parallel to
    but west of
Where the great river flows.

We drive the potholed road north:
Square waterlogged fields
Divided up by causeways where
Women carry bundles, here and there water spouts implaus-
    ibly from pipes, and a stray dog spars and squeals.

Little towns –
Tailors in dark huts,
Peddling mechanically, concentrating; a line of idle
    rickshaws;
Hens picking at straw, while their cock struts.

Krait

Dull ache of the noon sun,
Sullen drumming of the engine,
Lulling us to stupor …
A stabbed brake
And quake of scalding tyre on tarmac
Jabbed us awake. 'Snake,'
Spat our driver, jumped out
And was down on his knees at the front
While our eyelids were still
Only ajar. I clambered out,
Too. 'No – nowhere,' he cursed,
His mouth clenched,
And the Shiva flashes on his brow
Stretched and dropped.
I knelt, too, and looked about
And under the car. Nothing –
Not a breath of breeze
Even to stir the verge dust.
The journey resumed,
And I, curious, recalling
Kali, or snake omens,
Or Hindu veneration
For all things living, asked
Why he'd stopped so abruptly.
'Snakes.' He chewed the word.
'They get anywhere –
Drive shaft, steering column …
Then where are you?'
And I was appalled
That that was all.

*   *   *   *

On again: grey mudbanks, grey thatched shacks, pale yellow
    haystacks;
A stray egret unexpectedly takes off, flies …
Then – Kolkata,
And everything intensifies.

Kolkata

We Come to the City

We are tea leaves
Falling into the boiling kettle
Of Kolkata –

The butting and the pushing,
The hassling and the energy,
The screeching of traffic,
Honking, howling of car horns …

The pavements
Where Kolkata breathes:
Barbers shaving the hairy;
Shopkeepers cross-legged
On their counters;
Men, wary, round a square of sackcloth,
Slapping down greasy cards,
Staring, weary;
A skinny someone, legs like
Winter branches, squatting
By a tiny shrine;
In the gutter – heaps
Of unglazed terra-cotta smithereens,
Where the poor have drunk their *chai*.

Wood, cardboard, iron:
In the dusk light, shelters,
Dull scarlet flames bickering
At black bubbly pots;
Bedding, bushed and crumpled; bony people
Hunched under blankets … They steal
Half the pavement.

But only half – waves of walkers,
Like massing midges, scutter

In angry droves along, across, about the rest,
Till netted by the headlong clatter
Of taxis, rickshaws, bicycles,
Battalions of battered ancient buses.
They swarm
Till the roar and racket briefly rests,
Then surge – flies
Evading swatters.

Kolkata calibrated.

We're jostled, squeezed out, strained.
The brew is strong
And tasty.

Street Eats

Purses empty as our bellies,
We found a street food *wallah*
Mixing chowmein
Under a grey dusty banyan tree.
Eyes alive in his solemn face,
This cook went about his work
Like a conductor orchestrating Mozart.
Over yellow-flaring cooking flames,
Bright-mirrored in his stall's tin pots,
Bright in the traffic-swallowed,
Bus-rumbling, taxi-hooting night,
He worked, and we
Joined the little crowd
Crowding round him.
He stirred the big round tawa pan
With flat metal spatula,
Pitched in chopped chillies,
Shards of onion, a pinch or two
Of grated ginger, till it was

Soft, aromatic, steaming
To his satisfaction.
He looked up, ladled dollops
Onto pale plastic plates,
And six, nine, ten of us
Received ... and then
Hoiked forkfuls into mouths
Greedy as baby birds. And paid
A pittance, a mere
Tinkling of rupees.

After eating, I caught his eye,
Wanted to thank him,
But he was making chappatis
On a flat, black wok,
And flicked his eyes away, down.

A Shave

I sit square
On the flat stone
Before the squatting barber.
His face suggests a smile
As he tucks the faded cloth
Under my chin. For a moment
He contemplates my puny bristles,
Then takes scissors,
And clips and snips
Sideburns, a few stray whiskers
By my eyes, a stalk or two
Of nose hair ...
The lather swashed on cheek and chin
Is cool, sweet-smelling,
Inducing peace, till
He picks up his cutthroat
And goes to work.

His hands are gentle, I never fear
He'll slice me, draw my blood ...
He moves my head tactfully –
A butler straightening cutlery –
And his razor seems
Almost to caress
Till jowls, cheeks, upper lip
Are satin smooth, and soft.
The job is done.
Briefly he massages my face,
Drips on liquid, gently generates
An ice-cold, sealing balm,
And I stand up,
Fill his palm with rupees,
And walk away –
If not a new man,
At least cleansed a little,
A little purified.

Kali in Bengal

Kali Kutir

1
Kali kutir –
Kali's place, Kali's shrine.

Kali is the force of time,
The forbidden thing,
She who eats all
And licks up the drips of left-over blood.

Kali is patron of poets
Whose words go
Mounted on elephants.

In the pashmina night
Kali breathes;
On the cremation ghats
Kali is alive;
In the perfumed night
Kali is.

Her tongue is energy,
Her dance is danger,
Her heart blooms
In the five fists of the lotus flower.
She is the sport in creation,
She is the shadow in the feminine.

She is naked.
She is alive.

2

Kalighat –
The steps to Kali.

A seething anthill of urgent people,
Pushing, glancing, rushing, dancing,
Selfish, ashamed, gaunt, blamed,
Shove through the narrow chowks,
The crossings and covered alleys,
Where *boxwallahs*, pilgrims, stallholders,
Pedestrian pedlars pitch at you, offer
Plastic Kalis, Kali incense,
Veils, holy posters, chumpuk garlands,
Mystic, smoking, smouldering weeds …
Rickshaw men accost you,
Self-styled guides beguile you,
Smells, noise, spells, boys
Surround, seem to suffocate you …
It's bewitchment, it's
A bewildering beehive –
And you could be stung.

Mr Gautam Chatterjee

Was no ordinary
Run-of-the-mill guide
To Kali's temple.
While we were drowning
In the tidal waves of crowds
In chowks and alleyways,
He brandished his ID before us,
His Approved Guide's pale green card
(Photo enhanced), and bared
His white-tufted global belly
To display the sacred cotton threads
Which proved he was
Truly a Brahmin.
'Chatterjee, Bannerjee, Mukerjee –
Jee – that's how you tell a Brahmin.'

He processed our fascination
As if it were a row of beans
To be baked and canned.
First a glimpse of angry Kali
Enshrined behind a metal grille;
Then a sight of sacrificial goat,
Blood, slice, gore;
Here a dash of anguished pilgrim;
There some spice of serious *puja*.
Mr Chatterjee added
His own ingredients to the mix –
Homespun Hindu saws,
A sprinkle of holy water
(Direct from Mother Ganga's breasts)
Even a red and yellow thread
For us to keep.

At last he hung our flowery garlands
In an artificial tree fork, with a
'Sign your names, please,'
Pushing a gold-tooled Visitors Book at us,

And while we wrote, he lit a holy lamp
And muttered: 'Add
How much you'll give.'
We looked at him. 'Five thousand?'
Pause. 'Four and a half?'
(A little sadly), and led us
Towards the exit. 'Oh, and don't forget
Our shoe woman' – a hundred –
'My assistant' – two hundred –
'Me – no-one pays me, so – '
Five hundred. He accepted
The trifle as if
Welding a can lid,
Then scuttled away
To fish again among the thronging shoals,

While we departed,
Perhaps knowing a little more
About Kolkata's teeming poor.

Kali Mother

And Kali danced. Daughter of death, darling of darkness, she danced among gravestones, among dead men, on those whose time was gone. In her mind, it was midnight, it was moonless, day gone, death endless, so she danced.

Though Durga begged her – 'Finish ...' Durga, who had avoided death by her summons to Kali: Raktabija, demon, had racked Durga, downed her, and only Kali could help.

Kali had helped. She had rushed out of the tunnel of her darkness and grappled Raktabija and all his assistants. Her teeth flayed his flesh, her fingernails assailed his veins, and Kali sucked his blood, Raktabija's blood, and she swallowed his henchmen.

And then she danced on them, danced on the bodies on the field of her victory.

When Kali danced for you, you dreamed of dark, of despair and depravity. Her eye looked inward, but outwards at you, too. You couldn't avoid her temptation. Her head held high, her smile a tease, flung at your face. Round her neck silver bangles moved with her body's moving. She flaunted her naked breasts, round, heavy as ripe fruit, and her hips circled you. Her loose silky pants of gold and white, feathered and flared in the air. Silver anklets like breezes jingled in whispers. You were drawn to her like a sleepwalker when she danced, drunk on the blood she had spilled, she had drunk. Nothing could stop the delirium.

Till through the throbbing a baby cried. The sad gulp, the caught sob stopped Kali's possession. She paused, looked, saw the baby, and in a moment she had clutched up the little naked one and was holding it to her bare breast. Little pink lips closed over Kali's pink nipple like a flower closing at dusk.

Baby Shiva sucked, gurgled like the waters of the Brahmaputra, and a new world began.

The Little Goat

Tethered by a fraying brown string –
A kid, black coat, soft eyes, necklace
Of crimson roses, pretty as a nursery rhyme.
  So pretty the kid's life on this earth,
  So swift its end.

The kid treads daintily into the enclosure,
Its eyes seek, its sleek coat
Shiny as childhood, splendid as youth.
  So shiny the kid's life on this earth,
  So swift its end.

Father-like, a man gently lays its sweet head
In a contraption of poles –
Between two poles staked in the earth.
  So sweet the kid's life on this earth,
  So swift its end.

An iron bar slides slow down the poles,
Holds the kid's glossy head in its grip,
The father grasps ankles, legs stretch:
  So glossy the kid's life on this earth,
  So swift its end.

The axe whacks down on the kid's neck.
Its lost head skates on a spout of crimson.
Its pinned legs briefly kick – flop.
  So brief the kid's time on this earth,
  So swift its end.

Another Kolkata

The Great Tree*

Behind its green iron circular fence
The great tree stands.
No trunk – just roots and branches.
The jumbled, intertwining lattice work
Of verticals, diagonals, corkscrew curls
And drainpipe straights
Make a sort of spidersaurus,
Bodiless but with a thousand tentacle legs;
Or upside-down unmoving giant seaweed,
Fronds all muddled, tangled,
Entering and exiting themselves and others.
It is confined behind its green iron fence –
Yet even that, not so –

For some articulated growths have grown
Beyond, outside their cage, have grafted
Even past the path where we
Cicumambulate the so-called tree.

Nearby, young people in the sun
Frolic and have fun.
Shuttlecocks fly, laughter
Flits and spurts, and light
Splashes on rainbow saris
And cotton shirts.

But the great tree
Just stands, as if
Rooted in eternity, as if
This fantastic tangle –
So impossible, so fine –
Had just happened,
Without any cultivation
By the hands of time.

Rabindranath Tagore Concert

The young singer sits, leans
Towards his unseen inspiration,
And behind him his musicians –
Cymbals, drums, sitars, flute –
Flow and fall
In the lagoons and rapids of the melody.
It's a tide that tilts and trickles,
Tickling your inner ear
Till you hear the tingle of
The crisp northern winter,
The tips of spring's first buds,
Love that longs,
Is lost,
And stretches taut in lean goodbyes

That mean:
'Again ... come again ...'
– The soft sari of Bengal
Caught in a waft of air,
The unheard step
On the stair.

How Calcutta Became the Centre of a Great Empire

And now – we?
Pavement – goddess – snake or tree:
In this tangled tale
Are we merely outsiders, Britishers, and so beyond the city's
    pale?

The Ballad of Robert Clive

O, Robert Clive, our hero,
Won the hearts and minds of all
When he conquered Bengal province
And made its Nawab fall.
  I sing the song of empire
  To which we all aspire.

Siraj Din, the nawab,
Attacked the European trade,
And of glorious Calcutta
An Indian city made,
  And to avoid unwanted bloodshed
  Hid the whites who hadn't fled.

A hundred folks were locked up
In a small detention cell –
'The Black Hole' people called it,
The reason wasn't difficult to tell;
  For of those that entered there,
  Just a quarter breathed next morning's air.

Now some say Suraj Din
Knew nothing of all this,
But Clive and Admiral Watson
Didn't wait to find out this.
  'Revenge!' they thought – the utter
  Ruin of Indian Calcutta.

The nawab's mighty army
Marched past the British force,
And they glared and frowned and threatened
With footmen and with horse;
  But they didn't use their might
  Yet – the British didn't fight.

Thus – two armies waited,
Neither wanting to commence,
While their leaders sent out messengers
And the standoff stood off tense.
  And every word was double-edged,
  And every bet was hedged.

For Mir Jafar, the vizier,
Double-crossed the nawab's hand,
And Clive betrayed the trust
Of his trusting Umichand:
  Thought is made unruly
  When words are said untruly.

Now off towards the capital
Of the Nawab of Bengal
Bold Clive force-marched his soldiers

– They were ready for the brawl,
Till they stopped among the mangroves
And waited for their foes.

The heat was hot and hotter;
The air was moist and damp;
The monsoon broke and battered them,
And held them in its clamp;
  Oh, it was hot and sticky,
  That day at Indian Plassey.

Clive waited. Jafar wrote:
'Attack, and don't waste time.'
Clive sat beneath a mangrove,
Hoping for a sign:
  An hour he spent in thinking
  How to face his fate unblinking.

In seventeen fifty-seven
On the twenty-third of June,
The battle raged all day
Till the rising of the moon,
  And men were shot and killed
  And crimson blood was spilled.

Far away from where the bullets
Whizzed and flew and sang,
Jafar led Bengal's best soldiers
Away from where the clashes rang.
  Thus the nawab was betrayed,
  And the English victory made.

The nawab on a camel
Tried to work out his escape,
But Mir Jafar, once his ally,
Stepped in to change his fate.
  He stopped him on the way,
  And made his head to pay.

But Clive, the victor, smiled,
Made Mir Jafar Bengal's lord,
Then helped himself to riches
Which the land could not afford:
  He plucked out for himself
  The best of Bengal's wealth.*

Among his bloody soldiers
Half a million he spread,
And the Company's committee –
They were similarly fed:
  And the amount of looted gold
  Can never be truly told.

So Clive became a hero
By plundering and theft,
And poverty and misery
Was all he ever left.
  And thus was first addressed
  The high imperial quest.

Park Street Cemetery

Here everything's decaying,
Crumbling away
In silence.
The growls and snarls of carburettas
And squeals of beeping horns
Beyond the high stone walls
Are muffled; even
The scraggy croaking of the crows
Seems to dissolve
In this dry air.

Invisibly,
The huge mausolea
Crack, the dessicated funerary urns

Drift apart, subside
Like sighs.
They were promised remembrance
For eternity
For their civilizing mission –
W.C.Jones, Bengal Engineers, aged twenty-four,
Reverend Thomas Francis Hartwell,
Chaplain to this establishment, aged
Twenty-seven years and three months,
John Angus, Esquire,
Second Commissioner of the Court of Requests,
Mrs Amelia Hopkins, aged twenty-four,
Mrs Margaret Hollings, who
Lived respected and died lamented,
Mary Ann Samson, aged eleven months
And three days –
Now forgotten.

Time –
Up to his old tricks.

The certain assurance of Mrs M.A.Ladd
That the memory of her mother,
Mrs Ann McPhail, would remain
For ever sacred, the hope
Of George Thomson, senior merchant
Of the Bengal Civil Establishment
For everlasting life,
Dribbles away
Among the dead leaves, the collapsed tombs,
The fallen branches, cracking canopies,
Obelisks, graves
Of an age played out.

All's said.
Only squirrels scurry
Where the dust drops:
The remnants of the imperial quest
Lie broken, worn down, lost.

Park Street cemetery, Kolkata

Kolkata Normal

Kolkata has
Communist Party governance* – has had
For forty years. Perhaps
Kolkata is
Communism's last stand,
With its Lenin Sarani*, its Ho Chi Minh Sarani,
And its Cuban Revolution photo gallery
(With its own Communist Chairman
Shaking hands with Castro –
Or is it Ché Guevara?),
Bande Mataram become
Bande the defunct
Communist International.

108

Kolkata has
Beggars who nudge your elbow,
Beggars who jog your arm,
Beggars who hold out their palms
Like coconut shells,
Beggars who gently, slowly
Lift fingers towards lips,
Slow motion mime of dining:
Silent mouths, speaking eyes.
They're hungry.

Kolkata has
Men without legs,
Men without tongues,
Men whose eyes are empty holes,
Who walk past on stick limbs,
Skinny bodies wrapped in torn sacking
Loose as old men's jowls.

Kolkata has
Those who attempt
Their own version
Of Communism. Try.
Offer ten rupees
To the beggar boy with the smudged lip
And mouth pulled across his cheek:
He wants more –
For his sister, his mother,
His hunger, tomorrow …
He clings to your leg
Like a barnacle with steel arms,
Pays no heed to the reprimands
Of better-off, embarrassed locals
(Who probably vote Communist).

Another ten ignites
The quiet smile of the young mother,
Her dark-skinned near-naked child
Silent, wide-eyed on her hip.

The disabled woman sitting by the traffic fence,
Under a dust-drenched tamarisk,
Accepts her ten
Matter-of-factly:
It is her right.

And the scab-haired beggar girl who gets
A grimey, torn, old-minted note
Is desperate: she wants
A nice note, a clean note,
Not this tatty scrap.
You may say, insist,
It's still worth ten rupees.
She is unforgiving: she wants
A nice note, a clean note,
And only when she gets it
Do her grubby features blossom –
Her eyes burgeon, her sap of life
Flows. She legs it, off,
No longer professional beggar,
Now just a kid.

Kolkata has
All these, all
Communist citizens, and all
Normal – unique –
As us.

Moving North

Into Gorkhaland*

Where the far away mountains seem to be
Clouds in the soft warm morning,
You can hear the birds: black-naped monarchs,
Misty blue as the sky, tailorbirds, fussing, busy,

Babblers with staccato piercing '*Si-si-swi si-si-swi!*'
And green-tailed sunbirds, perched, alert.
The trees have flat tops, they're spindly, fresh green:
Sunlight flickers through them – sun shadow, sun shadow ...

Then it's drier. The earth is pallid,
Scrubby bushes, a cow or two,
And a wide, dry river bed, where the stones
Are white as bones, the earth pale parched,
And weeds cling to shaley banks.
Here, in this season, the river's
A path: women in threes and fours
Saunter along its arid track,
There's an old man squatting on his hunkers,
Sucking something, seeking nothing,
And a boy trying and failing
To bowl his hoop. Dusty potholes
Jolt the road, and on a high bridge
Over the waterless way
A hole yawns. Through it, you can see dry stones
Lifetimes below. Cars stop. Drivers
Ponder futures. We are no
High wire artistes. But our driver
Shakes his head. We creep
Onto the bridge, there's a jar,
A second when our imaginations race, and then
He accelerates away. Still alive!

A small man trudges past, leaning forward,
A bulging sack pulling on his broad forehead strap.
There's a smell of hay and wood smoke,
And fields of neat, trim tea bushes,
Enclosed by timber and wattle fences which
Couldn't keep a mongoose out.

We stop for *chai* at a roadside *daba**.
In the dark inside, men crowd round
An ancient dusky table top, polished by decades of elbows,
And roll dice. We grin and nod,

Ashamed we have no Bengali, no Nepalese,
As they climax with whoops and laughter.
We sip the sweet hot tea. A jeep
Bounces past, a lad on the tailgate
Clinging with one hand, waving at us
With the other, hollering. He jolts away.

We finish our drinks,
And follow,
North towards Darjeeling,
North into the mountains
Of Gorkhaland.

The Yak's Wool Shawl

In Darjeeling's Mall,
Where British gents and ladies
Once Sunday strolled,
Refugee Tibetan traders
Now set up their stalls.
While I stop to stare
At gimcrack woodcrafts,
You waste minutes by
A rainbow of shawls and scarfs
Displayed on a long iron gate
Before a locked-up shop.
In moments the female trader
Joins you, explains
The range of her rainbow:
Expensive silks and pashminas
To the right, simple sheep's wool, goat's wool
On the left. This saleswoman is
Shrewd and shabby,
With fish eyes and flat nose.
A little friendly talk,

A wayward chuckle,
And a fragile bridge is flung
Over continents, cultures.
You like a brown and pinkish shawl,
Finger it, and um. 'Yak's wool,'
She says. A smile. 'For you
Half price – it's Sunday,
And off-season … no trade.'
For a moment, just a moment,
Your eyes caress the shawl –
Then you remember
Your full rucksack, its weight
On your back. 'Maybe –
We'll come back tomorrow.'
'Tomorrow will not be here,'
Urgently. 'This shop' – pointing –
'Will be open then.' Her voice
Stretches taut
Like her hope,
And as we walk away, we catch
The eternal voiceless scream
Of the outcast.

*   *   *   *

Under the hovering Kanchenjunga range, Darjeeling's
    Chowrasta Square waits.
Monkeys race and leap, teasing stray dogs. The mountains
Lie still, like an old man in the top bunk. Is it merely legend
Which tells how when this sleeper wakes
The world will sink, black night will blanket all, all poetry
    will end?

The Old Man Sleeps in the Sun

The old man sleeps in the sun.
 He seems to float
Above the world, as if his race is run.

But when he wakes – night will cover all,
 The world will spin
Out of control, and humankind itself will fall.

Who is he? Maybe Shiva dreaming how
 To start again –
Improve the There-and-Then with a brand new Here-and-Now.

He may be Buddha floating there,
 Wondering how
Humanity may attain to a purer air.

But maybe that old man is you
 A very few years hence,
When all your world is torn in two,

When night strikes out your sunny day,
 There's only chaos,
And for you no longer any way.

The Last Steps

I put a foot wrong –
Our guide breaks off a pole,
Hands it to me. Now
My feet are more secure.
But it's a cumbrance
Through the bamboo forest,
Its brown earth and straight-growing shoots.
I hobble on. My foot aches

114

But my heart beats,
And not just from the work of climbing.
The forest wind breathes softly,
Once in a while you hear
A little river chuckling.
The quiet is like an old man
Sitting in his chair, watching time pass;
Yet it's green as youth.

We emerge
Where there's a square archway
And a tarmac road
Leading on, up.
Two carved and painted dragons
Seem to writhe alive,
One each side of the archway,
And under their fiery frown
Two women are at work:
They've lit a scrabble of sticks, and now
They're boiling up a bruised blue kettle,
Making *chai*, three rupees
Per little earthen cup.
We sit, drink, smell the breeze.

A boy on a motor bike
Skids to a stop, takes tea, too.
We smile a little, wonder how
To reach each other.
Coloured squares bob and yank
In the windy sunlight. 'Kites',
I say, pointing, but the boy
Snorts. 'Garbage', he says,
And more litter flutters
Prettily through the morning.
We laugh.

The last steps: we tramp
Up the metalled roadway to the top
Of Tiger Hill, look out.

There's hills twenty kilometres off,
Then a misty vacancy, then,
Adrift in the sky
Seventy kilometres distant,

Kanchenjunga range (the sleeping old man) seen from Darjeeling.

Kanchenjunga,
Beautiful monster,
And battalions of his supporters –
Kumbhakarna, Koktang, Frey's Peak,
Kabru, Guicha Peak, Simvo,
Panchim, Narching, Simiolchu …
Colossi in the still, soft morning.

They swim through the tides
Of the imagination –
Unassailable, impossible.
We turn away.
There is no passage here.
We must find another way.

Six : The Snake Uncoils

Another Beginning

We begin again – remembering we seek
Not just a cold, far distant place,
But stepping stones, a kind of
Imagination-washing chase.

Everything changes. We will
Add more spices to the feast:
Travel up incomparable holy Ganga
On our quest.

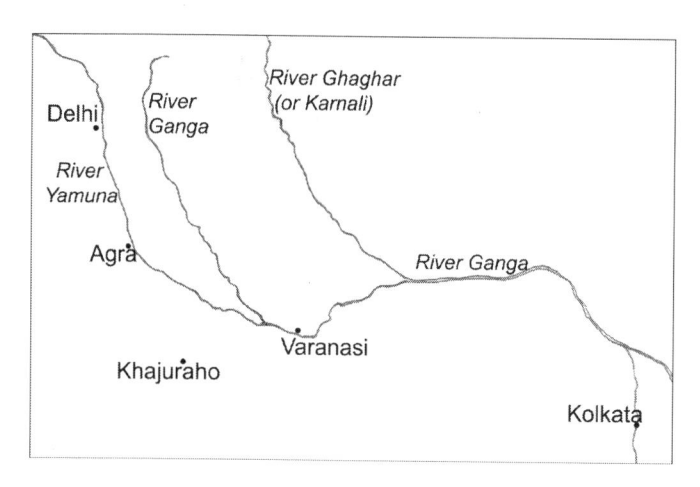

The plains of the River Ganga

The Girl in the Alleyway

It was in a grubby alleyway
That she approached – accosted – you.

Moving crab-wise,
But dancer-graceful,
Too-wise smile a shaft of brightness
On her cloud-banked face,
She stopped you. Rupees?
You had none. She begged
Foreign coins ... anything
To slake her mind-thirst,
Curiosity, brain brrr,
Coiled, snake-like,
And, snake-like, ready to dart.

And you:
'Why aren't you in school?'
She scoffed – hissed – her answer:
Hers
Were the grubby alleyways,
Dodging among tawdry shrines, souvenir stalls, *chai* shops.

So you –
To slake her thirst, perhaps, perhaps
Because she had a cobra's quick, light movement
(And brown velvet eyes of the muntjac)
Promised to bring her British coins
Tomorrow or next day.

You were busy tomorrow
And next day,
But one day some days later
You brought your pounds and pence to the alleyway.
She wasn't there.
There was a kind of vacancy
Among the trinket vendors and *chai* wallahs,
A sort of negative space.

She wasn't there next day,
Either. Or the next.
Was yours a promise broken?

Once you saw her –
Or thought you did –
Pursued by perhaps her father,
Arm raised to thrash.
But that was all.
And when we left,
The pounds and pence still snickered in your pocket.

Weeks later
You narrated to a friend the story of
The girl in the grubby alleyway.
Kindly he explained:
'Education? It's no use
To her. She's
Of the lowest cast,
Outcast. She
Can never escape
The life of a beggar.'

Never?
Will nothing
Ever change?

Shiva's City

But I say – not all
Is as it seems.
There is a reality
To be chiselled out of dreams.

The journey will
Tell all: we come to the holy city,
Pilgrims' paradise,
Signing the possible in impossibility.

Varanasi, Impossible City

In the spider's web of alleys, back lanes, chowks,
You're a fly. – And a fly would luxuriate
In this stinking Milky Way, these
Streets to the stars: faeces and urine,
Decomposing cauliflowers, garbage smouldering
In mustard-dark choke-smoke; exhaust fumes,
Animal smells, blocked-up drains ... and,
Where mourners tread, a burning pyre
Wafts slug-plumes from cremations.

Dunked in all this,
And in the noisy rampaging
Of jalopy horns, cruise barkers, motor choppers,
Saddhu salesmen, you can't hear
A fly buzz. 'We say in Varanasi –
No noise, no peace'. The tuk-tuk driver
Kicks his epigram
Like an accelerator, laughs,
And swervingly
Heads home.

Even the walls
Join the clatterballoo:
'GANPATI GUEST HOUSE' –
'SHIV GANGA SILK FACTORY' –
'DRINK PEPSI COLA'
In red capitals,
Repetitiously coarse.

Embarkations of tourists
Debouch on top of *dharma* seekers,
Pilgrims jostle touts,
Dogs whine, coins clink, and
On sopping artificial lotus leaves
Burnt-out holy candles drift.

The river pussyfoots past.

On it all, Shiva
(Blue-faced, trident-armed,
Conventional Shiva-of-the-pictures),
Stares. He's
Dead-eyed, for ever flat,
Stilled in his painted frame.

City of trash and ghostly hope,
Surely it's not possible.
Can this flat god,
This racketty hubbub, this creep of water
Point the star path?

Benares*, City of Dreams

Come to Benares,
  City of dreams,
Where nothing is something
  And what is is what seems.

Here beggars on street corners
  Cut quite a dash –
They're not asking for alms,
  They're offering you cash.

Scavengers haunt
  The city's waste ground,

Not to snitch for themselves,
But to return what they've found.

Bees create honey
  Without any hive,
And trees grow their fruit
  Before blossoms arrive.

Boats row themselves
  To the ghats on the banks;
They call out: 'We'll transport you!'
And they don't ask for thanks.

Here people are born old,
  But as time moves along
They grow to be children –
  And so ends this song.

Kashi*, City of Light

1
Kashi, luminous, light of the world.

City of gold, built on the Grand Trunk Road of the gods, egregious crossing place between earth and air, junction of the world and the heavens.

Before memories, beyond tomorrows, Kashi is caravanserai for life travellers – from the sweating heat of Kerala to the glaciers of the Himalaya; from the deserts of the Rajputs to the gates of Ganga; and from nearby, for those seeking only a way to go.

Kashi sits on Ganga like a morning vapour: the mists of unknowing, the colossal clouds beyond knowing.

Bathe, and be purified. Drink, and dissolve the debts of the
 flesh, debts of the soul.

Is it history? Is it legend? The sins of its citizens shifted
 Kashi's gold into stone, their wickedness changed the
 stone into clay, then the clay into mud. Does Kashi's
 mud shine in the sunlight, in the moonlight?

2

Shiva came to the city.
His search was atonement.
The snakes coiled in his hair raised their black heads, his
 strength stirred.

Shiva, the destroyer, created.
In a burst of flame, in a thrust of his *lingum*, he erected a new
 temple, Vishwanatha, the golden-roofed,
And he placed it near the temple of Kali of the cooking pot.

Shiva was exhausted by his labours.
He lay under a quince tree,
And cooled his *lingum* in the waters of Ganga.
And then he danced.
When he was rested, he danced the *tandava*, stamping,
 wailing, flailing his arms,
And the world rattled and shook like bamboo in a monsoon.

Shiva's dance encompassed the city.
He danced the golden age out and the stone age in.
He broke the tyranny of time.

Shiva left his city.
After him, the people went naked, they smeared their bodies
 with holy ash, and their hair was knotted like tree roots.
They were charged: deliver people from the agony of
 existence. Now they beg and bless.

Shiva, spirit of this misty place, pervasive, elusive,
This is your city, Shiva:
Power without effort, strength without tension,

Make possible the impossible.

Tourists

Varanasi – possible, impossible
Home on earth
To Shiva – hints
That more trembles, inches towards birth.

What now
Will Shiva show
As we descend like tourists
On the once-lost, lonely city of Khajuraho?.

Chausath Yogini*

Like the side-dish to a banquet,
Kali's Khajuraho temple
Is uncared-for, off the beaten way,
Run down. Yellow dirt road
To Chausath Yogini, pitted,
Winding through grumbles of rock,
The exposed broken bones of a world ignored.
And the destination's tumbled,
The shrines shrunk, lost or forgotten.

Stolid, empty granite faces
Stare gormlessly at
The open, weed-spread courtyard. They're like

Small grey hutches in a kiddies' zoo,
Turned to stone –
Stone thresholds, stone pillar posts,
Stone lintels – heaped-up, uncarved:
Is Durga here? And a stone tower
Tottering above each, empty,
Wind-fingered, dim.

One hutch, larger than the rest,
Is Kali's own.
A few smudged swastikas,
Some flowerheads, a sparse
Scattering of pods or seeds –
Scoria of a goddess
Gone elsewhere.

Outside, too,
Under the lumpish wall –
Emptiness, quiet – just
An anthill, pale earthy heap,
Asleep in the heat. Here, too,
The insect architects,
The navvies, brickies
Have long since scuttled off. Today
Its crusted pile is home only
To a sleeping cobra.
The hole where it slides in and out
Is black, silent.

The sun still shines.

* * * *

Is Kali then an outcast
From Khajuraho's Shiva, his tourist-tugging temples and
    shrines?
Is there no place for her
Among their towering splendours, their barely-symbolic
    signs?

We come to the field of temples armed with our imaginations
As well as guide books.
We seek poetry embedded in time-tangled art-architecture,
Believing it's there for whoever looks.

Sacred in Stone

Temple at Khajuraho

The Temple Without

The temples rise erect to heaven,
Sandy brown against the sky and grass;
Each one's a row of tapering pyramids,
Each pyramid's taller, statelier than the last.

Come closer. The shapely structures hold
Hundreds of fluid figures, carved fine as lace,
Each on its shadowed ledge, each row
Giving busy-ness to the building's every face.

Come closer still. The figures seem alive:
Naked couples face us, flaunt themselves;
Others perform gymnastically; some sway
Towards partners, others play with themselves.

Everywhere you look, lovers display their acts,
And we, by gazing, make their heaven our facts.

Carving on side of Khajuraho temple.

The Temple Within

Enter the temple under the latticed stone lintel.
The centre is a dance floor, under a sky-like dome.
It's square, pillared at the corners. On each side
Windows, and platforms for spectators on their thrones.

Beyond – the shrine, the womb chamber, encircled by
The parikrama passageway. Here worshippers walk round
The stone-enclosed *garbh-graha*, which contains
The Shiva *lingum*, in its *yoni*, standing proud.

Here Kali dances once again. Again
Shiva lies beneath her, and she, naked, stands,
Her feet astride his head, her face to his feet. He glimpses
Her barely-parted lips. She leans to take him in her hands,

Then swiftly turns, leads his dusk into her dawn,
And where his darkness melts within her light, poetry is born.

Shiva lingum in the inner sanctum (garbh-graha) in temple at Khajuraho.

Shiva's Song

I perform Shiva
I dance the *tandava* and shake the world

I perform Shiva
I am a poet, my dance is my poetry

I perform Shiva
I am a yogi, I contemplate patterns of worlds and words

Everything renews itself
I perform Shiva
I destroy everything and burn it to cinders. It smoulders to
    ash, fine ash

I perform Shiva
I dance on the ashes in the hearth. I kick up the ashes, let
    them fall where the wind blows.
This is my new world.

I perform Shiva
I bear no scales or sword
I wear no wig or robe
I see what you do, I do not ask why

I perform Shiva
I am the egret which flies over the dissolving world
I am the poet who sucks his pen and contemplates his new
    creation

I am the snake who slithers and stands erect
I am the destroyer and the creator
I am the performer of Shiva

You perform Kali
You are bone and being
I am no longer alone

Kali dances on Shiva: traditional image.

The Jewel in the Heart of the Lotus

Now no longer you and I

Beyond our bodies, we
Part the veils of apartness, turn
Trunk into snake
Sage into bayadere
Stone into bone

130

Sprinkle of wetness, sweet to the taste,
Vision cleansed, callow, the world
Clear new
Now
We see
Dew into puddle
Puddle into world-wetting river

And we weave our journey afresh

Dancer-rishi paddles
Up the spine-snake
Pirouettes
Where skull and skill converse

The meeting making
Music of silence, nirvana
Perhaps

   * * * *

Like tourists still, but also like
The cruiser bats of Kochi, glancing not left or right,
We bee-line for Agra,
Imperial capital of love and night,

Home to the Taj Mahal,
World symbol of undying passion,
Serene,
Beyond fashion.

Making Home

In the dusty afternoon
Where there's barely a drone
To disturb our plodding homeward –
Suddenly
A noise:
Squabbling infants? But dry-throated, batty ...

High in the boughs of trees,
Slung like canvas bags filled with cabbages
And swinging as if tweaked and twitted by a skittish breeze,
Bats – big as buckets ...
Flying foxes.

Question mark hooks
Tether bony bits to branches;
Leathery wings thrash, flutter, jerk;
Some unfurl like drab dishcloths;
Some squeal or cringe or nod or crash,
Find further resting-places, hanging spaces,
Flop or fly –
Graceful, ungainly colony
Shaking out,
Making home.

When the sun flicks them,
Their body fur flames
Bronze gold.
Then they're tangling and tumbling again,
And that glimpse beyond
Is told.

Prince Khurram and Arjumand Banu Begum

Lovers

The sun spat a ray. Dazzling.
The prince, fifteen years old, but already swaggering, felt his eye wince, glanced proprietorially at the offending stall.
Behind it sat a young lady, demure, yes, but still with a shadow of irony purling her lip.
The stall was unusual for the Meena Bazaar, the market attached to the royal harem in Agra. It sat just past the bend in the Yamuna River, below the imperial fort, but visible from this domineering building.
Mostly for sale were vegetables, shoes and clothing, pots, cutlery, household goods. This couldn't be a diamond.
'How much for this glass trinket?' the young prince, Khurram, asked with studied nonchalance.
'Diamond, not glass,' she corrected him.
She corrected him. But he was a prince. Curiously, though he was not to be corrected, yet he was not offended.
'How much?' he repeated.
Now her pretty mouth brought its smile out into the open.
'More than you can afford,' she murmured.
'Give her a thousand rupees.' He turned to a servant with a long leather purse. The servant, his face a studious blank, simply opened the purse and told out the prescribed amount.
Prince Khurram looked at the young stallkeeper. She accepted the money, and handed him the jewel.
Not that he needed it. He explained that to her with growing honesty. What he needed, he discovered as the conversation flickered and fizzed, threatened extinction, was her.
He may have been a mere fifteen. But he had met his destiny. And she? Who was she?

The next morning Prince Khurram entered his father, the Emperor Jahangir's marble-and-tapestried chamber.

Jahangir looked up from a dish of split peas and millet, laced with faluha. His moustache made a *moue*.
'I want to get married,' Prince Khurram erupted.
The Emperor raised a golden spoon of millety mush to his mouth.
'To whom?' he said.
'I met her yesterday. She's – '
'Yes? Who is she?'

Prince Khurram had to find out.

'She' was Arjumand Banu Begum. She had been born here in Agra, a year and a few months after his own birth.
She was the daughter of Asaf Khan, a high officer in the imperial household, and brother of Nur Jahan. Arjumand was therefore the Emperor's niece by marriage, for Nur Jahan was Jahangir's wife. His favourite wife.
So. Arjumand Banu Begum was a highly satisfactory wife for a Prince. Sighed relief.
Besides, she was beautiful. So beautiful, it was said, that the moon hid behind clouds when she walked in her garden. Another sigh.

For five years Prince Khurram courted Arjumand Banu Begum, while the court astrologers dithered, consulted their charts, stared at the stars and tried to agree the most propitious, the most auspicious day for their wedding.
And while they waited, Prince Khurram was married to two other princesses. No matter. That was what a Prince had to do.
His eyes were only for Arjumand.

And she learned his history, and as she learned it, she learned, too, to love him.
He was born on a warm January evening in the noble city of Lahore. On the sixth day after his birth, the Emperor Akbar, Akbar the Great, named him 'Khurram' – Joy.

In his childhood he was looked after mostly by one of Akbar's wives, Ruqaiya Begum, who had no children of her own.
Headstrong and capricious, his impertinence and his energy – he could run faster than any courtier's child – made him Akbar's favourite, made indeed the old Emperor uncharacteristically sentimental.
And when the old man lay dying, slowly sinking like a holed barge on a sleepy canal, it was the youthful Khurram, only thirteen years old, who sat by, holding his dry, leathery hand and offering a damp cloth for his sweaty forehead.

When she heard all this, Arjumand liked Khurram the better.
And she understood why he was his father's favourite son.

Five years eating the apple of love.
And then they were married.
Attended by nobles, zamindars, amirs. Soldiers – cavalrymen, infantry, mahouts in their howdahs.
Scarlet, purple, gold, cream.
Musicians playing *nanthunis*, *pulluva-veenas*, hammering on *tavils*.
Dancers in gauzy greens and golds; acrobats with oiled skins and shining plaits; caged panthers, porcupines and dry-humped dromedaries.
And crores of folk, all squealing and waving.

In the years that followed, the breath and hours of Arjumand and Khurram grew closer than the eyes of a tailor.
When Khurram fought the battles of his father, Arjumand went with him deep into the Deccan. And after campaigns which aggregated to the empire Mewar and Chitor, Mandu and Ajmar and the city of Ahmadnagar, Jahangir called him 'Shah Jahan' – King of the World.
And they were favoured by Jahangir's wife, Nur Jahan, too. The tall, stately queen, with her soft skin and black hair, who loved poetry and the dance, so reserved in public, so passionate in the arms of her Emperor, and so persuasive that soon she was the real ruler of the Empire.

She shared her counsel, not with the mercurial, opium-sozzled Jahangir, whom she loved, but with subtler brains, more audacious politicians: her parents, her brother Asaf Khan, her brother's daughter, Arjumand and Arjumand's husband, Khurram, the so-called King of the World.
Khurram was promoted and petted, flattered and admired. But all his care was always and only Arjumand.
If he was King of the World, she was the Jewel of the Palace – 'Mumtaz Mahal'. Her step was as the approach of spring, and her movement as the spring wind. And spring is a brief moment, therefore the most precious moment, in the Indian year.
She was as kind as the river which never runs dry. Many were the orphans and destitute children who felt the warmth of her waters as they flowed over them and bathed them.
She bore children of her own, but she never left her husband's side. Her presence feathered the eagle of his life. He gave himself to her, opened himself like a flower to the morning sun.
Their love watered India.

But in time Jahangir grew weak and weaker.
Who should succeed him?
Nur Jahan's parents had died. What would she do? Would she turn schemer? How keep alight the candelabra of her power?

Khurram and Arjumand talked, and the firelight drove shimmery shadows across their faces.
Together they talked, thought, decided.
To seize the prize before others could reach for it, before Nur Jahan could act.
Ten years after their marriage, they planted the ensign of defiance in the soil of the subcontinent.

Shah Jahan and Mumtaz Mahal, now at the head of a rebellious army, led their elephants and canonry at and into the imperial Moghul capital of Agra. They plundered and made chaos, till they were brought up flat against Agra Fort.

It was the first time this fort, this devil in Khurram's destiny, this thorn lodged in his life, blasted him. But not the last.
No sooner were they halted, than their tide was turned, and Arjumand and Khurram were forced to flee.
Across the swirling, white-dashed river Narmada the rebels struggled, the leather and steel of their batteries squeaking and clanging, their boots heavy with the water of defeat.
They were back in the Deccan. But there was no help here. Too many enemies.
They scuttled east to Orissa. Then north to Bihar.
Help? A straggle of discontented youth rallied to them. Call it an army? Call it men, reinforcements, would-be soldiers.
With the ragged defiance of these dregs of cast-out humanity, Khurram and Arjumand staggered Rohtas and Jaunpur, they laid hold on Benares, they wrung the scruff of Allahabad's neck.
But they were weary, and one night Arjumand noticed in her love a panting, a gasping of breath, and red eyes. His legs were swelling, his eyes appealing silently and desperately to her.
She pressed a fresh cloth to his temples. He groaned and rolled over. Her breath caught.
For a moment – all was lost.
And the ragamuffin army skedaddled.
Khurram's rebellious fever fought, and lost. A fortnight, and he could think to be King of the World again.
He knew he owed his recovery to his adored Arjumand.
That night, for the first time for weeks, they made love.

With Arjumand's advice and consent, Khurram sued for forgiveness.
Nur Jahan was near when the messenger dismounted at the Emperor's court. She listened to the message. She thought of her niece and her husband, and she thought of her own future.
Revenge withered in her throat.
An unusual compassion flowered.
And the Emperor, Khurram's father, forgave him his rebellion.

Khurram and Arjumand were ordered back to the Deccan, the hot, dust-curtained, featureless, cracked-out cauldron of the subcontinent, out of the way of court intrigue. It was hot there, it was dusty, it was dull.
But still, now the world knew who these two were. They knew who would be ready when the old emperor finally collapsed.
And the two still had each other. In the tired Deccan, their lovemaking was for ever fresh, their passion as alive as the sun-soaked lizard.
They proved it by the number of their children – ten or more by now.

The Emperor became enfeebled. He crawled off the stage of history, and into his magnificent mausoleum.
When a Moghul died, all his sons scrabbled for his throne. Like stray cats in a back alley – but worse, more vicious.
And this time was no different. But this time, one son and his wife had already shown they were poised and ready.
Prince Khurram, Shah Jahan, with the furtherance of Nur Jahan and her brother, speedily outwitted his siblings and claimed the throne for his own.
Now he was indeed King of the World, his world, and Lord of All Auspicious Conjunctions. And Arjumand was his lady. He allowed her control of the Imperial Seal. She approved his every Act.

On his succession, his bounty was unsurpassed. He granted riches, titles, robes of honour bedecked with fine jewels on his supporters, admirers and amirs. He cascaded gold and silver on the penurious and the destitute. And on Arjumand, the Jewel of his Palace, he bestowed two hundred thousand *ashrafis* and sixty thousand rupees. Her allowance, he decreed, would be no less than a million rupees a year.
And soon the new Emperor was back in the screaming heat of the Deccan. More fighting to be done.
Of course Arjumand was with him. Of course their lovemaking was passionate, perdurable, beguiling.
And more babies were born.

On the sixteenth of June 1631, Arjumand was taken to bed of her fourteenth child.
Khurram wandered the halls of the palace in Burhanpur, perfumed, bejewelled, impatient. He heard Arjumand's screams. He knew the midwives and nurses and doctors were sweating to sweeten her time.
He needed her. He wanted to discuss his wars. His plans. Which of his people needed support, which casting out. Their thoughts had always been one. She was his anchor, and now, anchorless, he was also rudderless.
Time drifted.
Women hurried by. They averted their eyes from the Emperor. They were busy.
Time dawdled.
Khurram sat down. He rubbed his eyes. He dwindled into sleep.

A scream awakened him.
Her scream.
There was a pause. He scratched his beard under his chin. He could hear nothing.
Two women hurried past. They didn't look at him.
And morning melted into noon. Then it was after noon. Then evening.
After thirty hours, there were further dreadful screams, more footsteps tapping by, doctors.
Khurram stood up. Held his breath.
One – two – three –
Till a woman came painfully towards him.
She walked so slowly.
She looked at his feet.
'The Empress – '
'Yes?'
'Is dead.'
And the moon scowled into darkness.*

The Illumined Tomb

Stone stone stone stone
Shah Jahan ate the dirt of grief.
For a week no-one saw him. No tap at his door was answered.
No sound stole from behind his lock and bolt.
People began to fear: was the Emperor dead?
The Emperor was not dead. He had a duty to his God to perform his role as Emperor. The performance was not over.
At the end of a week he came slowly over the threshold of calamity. He could barely see his way, the quick of his eyes were raw with weeping.
He ordered the body of his Jewel to be interred in Zainabad, her walled pleasure garden where she had walked.
And he ordered millet and chick peas.

Even as he took up again the scrolls of governance, Shah Jahan's mind was sparking an idea. To build her a fitting memorial. A place of peace. A tomb to outlast time.
Hubris?
Perhaps.
Can love outlast the aeons? Is it a dagger to defeat the reverseless ticking of time?
He remembered the Meena Bazaar in his capital city of Agra. He would build there, where first their eyes had crossed, and been bedazzled. Thus would time be reversed.

In a year the building began.
In that year, Shah Jahan's hair turned ashen.
But his troubles were to be weighed against the tomb of his imagination, peace's place.

The body of his beloved was brought back to Agra, her birthplace. It rested on the banks of the Yamuna.
It seemed she was overseeing the building of the mausoleum.
The Illumined Tomb, Shah Jahan called it.

Three acres of the old bazaar were ploughed up. Stones and rubble were poured in. Then the area was levelled.

Shah Jahan's weakened eyes could not properly see to the work. His managers, Mir Abdul Karim and Mukkarimet Khan, did that for him, as the brick scaffolding (no common scaffold poles here) was erected, the road to be used to drag in the building materials was laid, and teams of twenty and thirty oxen were hired for the work.

Water from the Yamuna River was drawn up by ropes and buckets pulled by lines of horses, and stored in grand tanks.

Shah Jahan could not watch.

He returned to the Deccan, fighting, wreaking chaos to match the chaos of his heart, beating down the forces that would drag him back from his grief.

The kingdom of Ahmadnagar was destroyed.

He wore spectacles for his raw, salt-rubbed eyes.

The fighting went on.

Stone stone stone stone

Marble was the key. Marble for calm. The tomb must be made of white marble.

They raided the land of the Rajputs for the finest white marble in the world. Pure, snow white, imperishable.

First it formed the huge plinth on which the tomb would stand. At each corner of the plinth, tall tapering minarets in white marble rose.

In the centre, the chamber which would receive Mumtaz's coffin was to be of white marble, too.

Above the chamber, the great white dome. The designer, Ismail Afandi, made it seem taller by setting it on a drum-like construction, a 'false' base.

And he added four smaller domes, all white marble too, at the corners of the chamber.

The top of the dome bore a lotus design, repeated on the minarets and lesser domes.

Finally, at the very apex, a golden finial spired upwards, upwards, crossed by a crescent moon whose horns, too, pointed upwards. Were the horns and spire designed by Qasim Khan to resemble Shiva's trident?

Whoever watched the building was astounded.

The white marble was decorated with jasper, shaped into letters, the calligraphy of the renowned penman, Amanat Khan, and inlaid in the white marble panels. Ninety-nine names for God were thus inscribed on the tomb.
Inside the octagonal chamber, the inlay was of different, various gemstones.
The space for the coffin of the dead queen faced Mecca.

Shah Jahan shut his weary eyes.
His back was bent now, his neck flesh hanging loose like an empty purse, his face cut with wrinkles.
He drove his army north, beyond the Khyber Pass, conquering, slaughtering.
But he had no-one now to share his tent, no face opposite his to be lit by the fitful flames, no partner to plan and plot and push out new ideas, no presence across the lamplit dinner table when weary with the work he longed for companionship. He was alone.
Only the building of the Illumined Tomb sped on gladly.
Only here was peace planted.
Now they laid out the mausoleum's garden. Straight, elevated pathways passed through beds of roses and daffodils, past ensembles of fruit trees.
In the centre – the Pool of Abundance, a perfect liquid mirror. Four streams led out from the centre: the four rivers of Paradise, some said, but others saw the four rivers of the world with the central pool Lake Mansarovar.
At night the moon silvered the water. It was white as the marble.

'I have no taste for ruling,' said Shah Jahan. 'The savour of life is dull on my tongue. No person delights me, either.'
His preferred company was Mumtaz' and his eldest daughter, Jahanara Begum.

The walls of the campus were of red sandstone. The gateway of marble, echoing the pattern and the motifs of the tomb itself.
To the west – a mosque. To the east – a guest house. Mirror images of each other.

Sixteen summers burned away, sixteen dull winters shifted into spring, and the Illumined Tomb was done. Tranquility could begin.

The marble, the gems and precious stones, lapis lazuli, sapphire, jade, turquoise, crystal from the world's most exotic hiding places were now set, unmoved, unmoveable, in the pristine architecture. Was time stopped?
When the Emperor announced at the completion of the building that anyone who removed a single brick from the high heavy scaffolding might keep what he took, the whole huge structure was dismantled in a single night.
When he determined that nothing should ever be made to equal the Illumined Tomb for his only beloved, Ismail Afandi's right hand was cut off to ensure it.
Yet he hankered to perfect perfection. A black mausoleum of the same magnificence across the Yamuna River, he and she sleeping, eternally at peace, but linked eternally by a bridge over the water, the yin and yang of life and death, could be ...
But never was.

The Straitjacket of Nothingness

The Illumined Tomb – symbol of serenity, honey after the bitter vinegar of life ... yet for Shah Jahan it broke the string of his long song.
After it was completed – what was there to do?
Was it madness that supervened?
He began a mad building spree – a pearl mosque; then the Red Fort in the old capital, its centre the exorbitant Peacock Throne; and finally a whole city, Shahjahanabad, with wide

streets, admirable chowks and the largest mosque ever seen in India, the Jama Masjid. A new Delhi bedizened.

And he began a mad sexual spree, indulging the appetite which Mumtaz alone had satiated with all sorts of concubines and courtesans, *nautch* girls and harlots, and even a bevy of new wives. No woman was safe from his new-discovered lechery, and he resorted to all manner of aphrodisiacs to sustain his appetite.

In the autumn of the year which marked his three decades as Emperor, he tottered, fell over. Too much, too much.
Fever reddened his throat and chest, and the sweat dripped like rain. His legs swelled like gigantic bolsters. His agony screamed.
And rumour, like a black forked tongue, spat out its poison: 'The Emperor is dead. Who comes next?'

But the Emperor was not dead. Coddled by his favourite daughter, Jahanara Begum, overseen by his aesthete elder son, Dara, and sipping only mint and powdered millet soup, the old man – for that's what he was now – slowly crept towards health.

Too late.
The river of time was tumbling over new rapids. The Emperor's vulture sons were flying.
Armies gathered. Men marched. In forge and factory, steel was hammered into swords, arrow shafts were shaved, chains made into mail.
It was too late.

Shah Jahan cowered. Where was the strut and swagger of the King of the World? Gone in a shiver!
He cowered.
He trusted his eldest son, Dara. Dara must set to and defend the Empire.
When the host of the defenders was drawn up, Dara turned to his father, who caught him in a clutched embrace. He held on, his face fast in the young prince's shoulder.

When he drew back, his lashes, cheeks were wet.
And Dara went out to his doom.

Was it a week? Two weeks? Who counts time when those kestrels of fate, life and death, hover together and beat the air?
News came.
Dara's defeat.
Dara's humiliation.
And his conqueror? Shah Jahan and Mumtaz Mahal's third son, Aurangzeb, now galloping towards Agra.
Aurangzeb, brimful of energy, greedy with self, fast friend of fate, the new fate, the fate that he himself would make.

Shah Jahan quailed in Agra Fort.
Big bolts shuttered.
Arrow slits were manned.
Shields thrust up.
When Aurangzeb arrived, he took stock of the place.
A little laugh burbled, and he ordered the water supply to the fort cut off. The defenders were to go dry. The little laugh, no more than a giggle ...
In three days, their surrender was settled.

Son, my son,
Fate doesn't heed lamentations or complaints:
Not a leaf falls without its destiny.
Once my army numbered tens of thousands.
Now I lack even a cup of water to drink.
But in your prosperity
Don't always lean on
Luck.

He admitted Aurangzeb's ambassador – his grandson. Mohammed Sultan,
Who brought the old man crystallised fruits, wine in bottles, a velvet-lined box with bright-coloured *barfi** in edible foil.
The old man accepted.

Then Mohammed Sultan locked the door on him, confined him to his chamber, and seized his papers, his seal, his resources.
And left.

And left a squadron of guards to guard the fort.
Agra Fort. Shah Jahan's nemesis.

Never again did Aurangzeb and Shah Jahan set eyes on each other. Never again did the father hear his son's fatuous giggle. There were no more meetings.
When the new Emperor had Dara, his brother, executed, he sent Shah Jahan the head in a bag. He himself remained aloof.
Shah Jahan shrieked. But he could not die, could not find peace.
He was cabined in his chamber. There was no escape.
Years passed.

It was the high day of hopelessness.
And he had thought he was lonely before!

Like paint in a paintbox
My sky comes in squares.
But the squares are all blue.
I lie on the board floor, wait
For a kite, a pigeon, a small winter wren –
Nothing comes.
Or get up, grasp the bars,
Shake and shake.

And don't look
Down river.

I gaze on
Grey sandy ground
With a stubble of rocks,
A few green tufts
Skulking in crevices.

Further up
On the almost-island in the curve of the river,
A man in blue with a stick
Advances. His gaggle of goats
Gaze mournfully at him, rolling their heads.
Beyond,
Four or five people,
Bright saris, turbans, sit
And stare.
Where can they go?

The river reflects emptiness.
The sky is empty.

And then at last I dare to look –
The far white marble,
Stone stone stone stone
Perfection echoing hers,
Palace of peace,
Minarets, arches, domes,
Endlessly varied, yet all
White as adamant,
Familiar, yet strange
As we were.
And the gold points
Aimed at the sky,
The whole sky.

Bird, bird,
You are bred to escape
The harness of days,
The straitjacket of nothingness.

When Prince Khurram died, there was no ceremonial funeral.
His only living son, Aurangzeb, was not present.
The corpse was washed, and laid in a sandalwood coffin.
A barge slowly carried it the yards down the Yamuna
And it was laid in the Illumined Tomb

Beside that of Arjumand Banu Begum,
His beloved.
Was peace here? Was time reversed?

The Illumined Tomb, the Taj Mahal, withholds that secret.

Up River to Delhi

We ask: what did Agra add to Khajuraho's passion?
Was the journey thither
Worth facing, outfacing the pestilential, buttonholing, trinket-
    touting swarms?
Shaking out, maybe; making home, maybe; an alternative,
    perhaps, to wild-goose-chasing dither?

Yes. After the tantric ecstasy,
A different flame:
Silence grows from hot entanglement
As the flower from the stem.

Noiselessness nudges us up river to Delhi:
Here perhaps to finesse
With passion or poetry, or wisdom's dance,
The beating recurrent head- or heart-guiltiness.

We sigh. It's warm. Streets, once plunging fury,
Now offer up home, hearth.
We settle here –
Sparrows in a dust bath.

Sri Niwas Puri*
(*residential district in Delhi*)

The morning sings
With chants of *boxwallahs*:
'Eee tarry-a-deee' – The veg man,
Droopy moustache, droopy eyelids,
Fills the street with music.
He leans on his bike,
Idly builds towers in his trailer
Of cauliflowers, cabbages, beans.
'Tilly lolly lolly tilly oo-er'.
Is this the fresh fish seller
With his handcart? Or the banana man,
His goods already blackening
In the long, strong sun?
The man selling sugar cane cubes
Is a bass, the woman
With the tower of shiny pots and pans
Balanced like a batty bird's nest
On her head, sings
A high, drifting melody
And smiles as I pass by.

Sachin in the Internet café
Laughs at me, calls me
'Grandpa poet', and insists
I sit at his computer
In the window, laughs again
When unwary customers ask
Me if they can use some cyber space.
Mr Sandeep, our *dhobi wallah*,
Teaches me the Hindi for 'Hello' –
'Ram ram'. And when I've left our dirties
In his care, I ask (naive as new-washed knickers)
'What's goodbye?' 'Goodbye? – Same –
Ram ram.' 'Ram ram?' I repeat. 'Again?'
We laugh. I stumble on.
Mr Chhabra sells us

Kitchen towel and toilet roll.
He speaks good English, insists
We go home. He'll have delivered
What we've bought (though
It's only twenty yards
And we will have to
Tip the delivery boy ...)

At the junction half a dozen women
Crowd a ropey charpoy,
Feet bare, worn chappals dropped beside
The rough-wood bed's leg.
They chatter like mynas, bobbing, pecking,
Hopping from topic to topic,
And their laughter, too,
Is one of the street's songs.
They are dressing one another's hair,
Combing out long white tresses like breaking waves
In the bronze evening light.

At night, at last, the street symphony slows.
A group of lads laugh loudly
Somewhere down the road, the last motor-bike
Rasps past, the grandmother, singing softly,
Sighs into silence ...
                      ... and then you hear
The slow, shuffly steps of the *chowkidar**,
The hollow clatter of his staff on the road,
His shrill drilling whistle. He could be danger,
Stalking the night, an echo unseen,
But he's part of our orchestra
Whose theme means – All's well
In Sri Niwas Puri.

        *   *   *   *

If the journey is to drain
The poison from the waste of years,
I – we –
Must pierce the skin of time, the scald of tears.

Delhi, city of poets,
Admits us to itself,
Gives space
To seek the breadth and breath of lifewealth.

In the Shrine of the Sufi Saint, Hazrat Nizamuddin*, and his Poet, Amir Khusrau*

Gold gold gold
Beyond the railing
The people wailing

The men stoop and sob
('No ladies allowed inside')
There is an air of awe
There is a ceiling and a door
And gold
And emerald green edged with gold

White bulbous dome
Over the home
The small room
The all room
Of the dead Sufi saint

White dome-shaped railings at the roof's edge
Over Hazrat Nizamuddin
His earthly relics

Men shuffle round the covered coffin-like trunk
Sunk
Under the gold green white dome

Home
To a dead man

'No ladies allowed inside'

And beyond –
Khusrau
His remains

And the pain
And men shuffling round
Muffling breathing
Gasping sighing
Tying covers over the humped coffin-like thing
In the centre of the little cabin
Green cloth
Gold edged
Lowering flowers
Seeds in plastic bags
Needs needs needs

And a drift of incense pulling and felling the senses

In the centre of the little cabin
He lies
He dies
Himself a saint
Stored
Adored

Abroad
For poetry
For music
For the poet magus
Who danced

'The river of love flows uphill:
If you jump in, you'll drown;
If you drown, you'll get to the other side.'*

Word text
Who is to steal the meaning?
Who is to budge the image?

Women men
Song sung danced

And the body may not be there
And the spirit may not be there
Water poem
Drowning swimming

Gold gold gold
Beyond

Sons of Khusrau
(Being the Diary of an Aspiring Poet in the Time of the Emperor Bahadur Shah II*)

29 August 1856
Dared to go to the *mushairah** (poetry evening) at the house of Mamnun, well-known poet. (Mamnun is his pen-name: all poets have pen-names – Azurda, Nayyir, Jauhar ...)
The room was filling when I arrived. The lamps all round gave a coppery glow – low tables, musical instruments, playing cards, a backgammon board.
Two or three women, astoundingly beautiful, sat together, talking quietly, smiling and greeting the men.
Hubble-bubble pipes puffed grey clouds. Incense drifted.

The subject for tonight: Love. I was prepared.

But who recites first? A place of esteem. Debate.
The first and the last are the coveted times to recite.
The *shama*, the tall wax candle placed before whichever poet has been chosen by our host, is taken round the room, and set

down in front of *ustad** Sebhai, whom we venerate because he writes in Persian as well as Urdu.
Tonight – heaven be praised! – he is in Urdu.

> *Your heart is entangled in her tresses,*

he intones, almost singing. His verse plays with the image over twenty, forty couplets. He ends:

> *Her heart is as tangled as her hair.*

There is approval, boisterous calling out. 'Vah vah! Vah vah!' 'Subhan Allah!'*
Then the sitar plays, two women dance. The huqqas burn. Wine spills from flasks, cup meets cup, faces come alive, are full of light.

The poetry continues.
A poet with chunky white beard and mournful shoulders stands:

> *If there's nothing in this encounter,*
> *Why do our eyes keep meeting?*

he asks. There's desperation there. I see some eyes meeting across the room. He continues:

> *Don't talk to her. Do you trust yourself?*

and

> *By the time my scratches have healed,*
> *Your nails will have grown again.*

Is he sincere? Or just clever? Is this performance the truth? Or is he merely going through the motions, amusing himself?

> *She came to know how I enjoy*
> *The tortures she inflicts –*

he's ending now –

Now
She just leaves me alone.

And there's silence. Then acclaim. 'Vah vah! Vah vah!' again. And 'What art! What eloquence!' He smiles, shrugs his mournful shoulders, subsides.
More wine is poured. Goblin faces, fragrant hair flowing in tides, dark playful eyes. And again music, dancing. How the incense leads to embraces.

We'll meet again – on Doomsday,
You said, as you walked away.
I pondered – could there be
Another like today?

The chink of the glass, light leaping from the rim.

The gates of mercy are not closed
Though the door of the tavern is open.

Now the *shama* is set down before me. The flame leaps a little, like the heart on seeing the beloved, and sinks and is still.
Memory is like a cloud. My feet, my fingers tingled. I performed, but I can hardly remember performing. The lamps fizzed, smoke floated, trembling across me, but I spoke – with passion, with truth. I stood before my peers and recited.
Then, the voices of approval – 'Vah vah! Subhan Allah!' – and hands reaching for me, a glass of wine thrust into my grasp.
I sat. A young woman held my arm. I could feel my chest muscles slacken.

When I looked up again, the candle flame stood before a poet with a hook nose and long black greasy hair.

*Love gives an ache which can't be cured,
Yet cures every ache.*

An adept at paradox, obviously. And later:

*I can't survive without love,
But love is killing me.*

The night slunk away. Fast now, faster. My beating heart was calm. Dread and desire alike – done for, defeated. The lamps gutter, but there is light in the poetry. The voices, the melodies make the room glitter and glow. Words of joy, words of grief. Love in darkened niches.
The last poet is Mustapha Khan who has just returned from Calcutta. He is known as Shaftar. He speaks. He sits. A bubbling up of voices, but slower, more melancholy.
The last glass, the last puff of the hubble-bubble ganj, the last kiss.

Outside, dawn streaks the east in careless watercolour.
I am a poet.

6 September 1856
The candle which burned like the muse through the ecstatic night of longing and poetry is now black wick. But not everything is dead.
Today came a message. I am invited to the next Royal Mushairah, to be held in the Diwan-i-Am, the Hall of Public Audience, in the Red Palace, on 15 October – little over a month from today.
The prescribed topic – movement and stillness.
It's not clear whether the movement has to be physical or emotional. Or mental, perhaps. Metaphor, image, rhythm. Catch the flight of unseeing.

Poetic talent receives its severest test at the royal mushairahs. Poets will gather like a flock of birds in barley. They will compete with one another. Even the Emperor himself, Bahadur Shah II, competes.

His poetry is also poetry.
He is a poet among poets.

This is life within the circle, a measureless, dateless world.
For a gulp of wine, the poet gives a decorated fantasy, or heartbreak unbound.

7 September 1856
Flower Festival. An opportunity to make verses.

All Dehli* follows
The Emperor's procession.
Slim and tall like pasture grass,
Dressed in green like early summer pasture grass,
He leads, proceeds
Through his own gold, old city,
Permitting, admitting
The shouts and applause
Of his playful people.

The flower canopy
Bobs through zigzag streets –
Yellow, orange, green, white –
Through the old city, the dirty city,
The city that cannot be.
Past the pigeon-chested red-and-white womb tomb
Cuddling the Father of the Mughals*;
Past the thronging merchants and mendicants,
The noise, the hymning, and clatter of begging bowls
Girdling the fat round onion and squat pale pillars
Of Sufi saint, Nizamuddin's velvet-clothed coffin;
At last to the boastful Safdarjung's sepulchre*,
Big, bold, fanciful.

Picnic.
Wine, pakoras, fish and fowl.
And green grass,
Green trees,
Wide orange pathways.

And on,
With rattling and rolling jog,
All Dehli on holiday,
Even the Emperor –
Though when he peers down from his howdah
His dignity sits firm in its saddle.
The elephants loom
Over palanquins and people,
Horses and bullock carts,
Soldiers and trumpeters.
The royal pigeons in their jewel-studded cages
Look startled when their elephant
Misses a step, bumbles.

Moslem, Hindu, poet, people,
Emperor and commoner, come
To kick up their heels and cavort.

8 September 1856
The Emperor, who is also the tragic poet, Zafar, loves his food, his wine.
Today – another picnic. The Emperor ate mangoes, removing the stones from his mouth with decorum, and watched groups of beautiful women singing, dancing.
Later he visited their curtained pavilion. He stayed for more than two hours.

This evening I met a palace servant. I am curious about this old man, supposedly our Emperor – poet, scholar, patron of the arts. He seems less interested in power than in playing chess or cards. He flies kites for amusement. Who is he? What is he?
'Nothing,' says my man, clicking his tongue on the roof of his mouth. 'Sometimes he don't even pay us our wages, what's due to us.'
'But he has – '

'Nothing,' says the man again. He picks his teeth as my look quizzes him. 'He's nothing. He's just a shadow, an idea. That's what all the poetry's about. Where's the life?'
He shambles off into the night.

Bahadur Shah II
'Zafar'

9 September 1856
The procession moved on again today. Through the Mehrauli bazaar to Jogamaya temple, built by our Emperor's father thirty or forty years ago. But it's on the place where an ancient temple of the yoginis once stood. Can one feel the spirit of the ancient almost-divine female followers of Kali in us today? Should we feel it?

10 September 1856
A day of sports – quail fighting, partridge fighting, cock fighting – and spectacle. Teams of strong men tug a huge rope to discover which is the strongest. There are postures and *tableaux vivants*. Displays of horse-riding and fencing. The elephant parade, the giant tuskers all caparisoned like ponies in a circus. And soldiers in colourful uniforms (hardly practical for fighting) parading up and down and past the Emperor, who smiles and puffs at his huqqa.
Musicians keep up the spirits. I notice that two or even three of their songs are written by poets of our time. I think one is by none other than Zafar himself.

11 September 1856
The procession moves on again, this time to the tomb of Qutb Sahib. Originally this grave was just a mound, grass-covered, but now a marble paling surrounds it and on one wall there is a superb mosaic of flowers. Perhaps this is the origin of our

Flower Festival, for this is as far as the procession goes, and here the canopy of flowers is laid.

The *Dargah** here also contains the beautiful Pearl Mosque, and the gateway we have learned to call 'Zafar Mahal' since our Emperor had it rebuilt.

Among the graves in the *Dargah* is one unfilled – it awaits Bahadur Shah II, Zafar. It is in a quiet, shy part of the garden, somewhere to lie peacefully after all the poetry has been written.

14 September 1856
This evening I met two of Dehli's poets. (There are so many poets – is there room for me?) Talking is different from hearing the poets recite. You learn what goes on *round* poetry.

First they talked about the *ghazal*, Dehli's favourite form, and how its couplets must be linked thematically, not sequentially or logically, how the last couplet should incorporate the poet's pen-name in a kind of pun. That's why they (we?) have pen-names. The Emperor is 'Zafar', the victorious one (though his poetry is tragic rather than victorious). The greatest poet of our time is 'Ghalib', the pre-eminent one, pre-eminent, I suppose, in subtle philosophical thought. Sometimes, I must say, his philosophical subtleties are hard to unravel!

'What do you gain from being a poet?' Dil-Aram, the first poet, asked. 'Fame after you've gone? And what good is that if you want to buy a glass of wine today?'

Still, they see themselves as sons of Khusrau, the medieval poet, singer, songwriter, who invented the sitar, and whose verse is still sung.

Our Emperor would patronise the living poets of Dehli if he could, like the emperors of old. No-one doubts that. But he is destitute, a pauper. 'Compare that,' said Raqam, the other poet, 'with his ancestor, Shah Jahan. When he was Emperor, he'd weigh his favourite poet, Saib of Tabriz, and give him his weight in gold.'

'The stars stay in the sky,' said Dil-Aram. 'Why worry? If this doesn't happen, that will.'

'In the garden of life, who are the bulbuls, the nightingales?' rejoined the other.

They discussed Zafar's poetry. It's intricate, convoluted even, full of melancholy. Love, pain, sorrow. But with a streak of mysticism. Ghalib*, his master, and he meet regularly to discuss his work, but they don't always see eye to eye.

'Is poetry a matter of rhyme and rhythm?' asks Ghalib, 'or thought and meaning?'

Practicing poetry might be harder than I imagined.

27 September 1856
Another *mushairah*.
I followed the lights all the way up the narrow crowded *koochah** to the house of Lala Balmukand Hazur, our host. He is an old man, serene, almost prophetlike, and the people who throng the lane, having heard of his *mushairah*, long to see the poets arriving.*
The chamber within is decorated from niche to niche, but unlike the lane outside, it is dark, smoky with incense. Flowers, everything beautiful. Music offering its own sensual draughts, a paradise captivating eye, ear. The bolsters which the poets lean on are burnished, heavy, bejewelled.
A feast of verse and food. Poetry – rhythm *and* thought.
It's night – stars – the figures are like statues, sculptures lost in time.
Wine in the glass, dreams in the mysterious night.
A dark eye, and long black hair falling like water over shoulder blades, spine.
We drank all night, and the wine was sweet.
In the morning, the rain washed us clean.

Where is the ecstasy? The spires of last night?
A burnt-out taper, a broken heart, a singed cloth.

1 October 1856
Looking for inspiration I wander the streets of Dehli.
On the steps of the Jama Masjid, the story-tellers make their hearers' eyes shine.
In Chandni Chowk*, knots and groups of people talk, argue, sing, recite. Poetry, politics, philosophy.
They munch fruit, kebabs, pakoras from pavement stalls. Or watch the quick-change artists, the acrobats, puppet men, jugglers.
The men have long hair and beards. Most women are in purdah. The clothes are bright, there are caps and turbans.
And they must shift when bullock carts approach, or a British carriage, with stiff-backed official and guard of rough redcoats.
For those in despair, there are astrologers, for those in pain mountebanks and quack remedies.
From this crowded world, the poetry of a people grows. And I think I have my poem for the royal *mushairah*.

15 October 1856
The Royal *Mushairah*.
The Emperor Bahadur Shah II, 'Zafar', presides. He sits on a central dais in the Diwan-i-Am under a green-and-gold canopy and lights the ceremonial upstanding *shama*.
He himself recites first. His old face is wrinkled with sadness, brown like an autumn leaf, but his voice is still fresh, its tones and rhythms vigorous.

> *Life is a flash of lightning –*
> *But there's still time*
> *For your heart to bleed.*

What you notice about him is his correctness, his refined manners, his *politesse*. He asks for contributions with charm and an extremely mild sense of irony. It's so delicate, you hardly notice it.

Paradox prevails.

Outside, Chandni Chowk and the Red Fort are bedecked with a thousand bright-burning lamps and candles, and crowds saunter and stare. But within, there are lumps of lumber under dustsheets, junk piled higgledy-piggledy in corners and against walls. Dust lies thick in places, and the walls are streaked with dirt as if the ceilings wept.
Still, in the Diwan-i-Am, an effort has been made, you can see that. There are Chinese lanterns, chandeliers, candelabra, so that the place is a bubble of brilliance.
From the roof, streamers of jasmine dangle. Between the double red stone pillars with their scalloped arches are looped more streamers of flowers.
Servants stand with eager eyes and folded hands. There is wine in jugs, each place is marked by a silver goblet, and there are rows of polished huqqas. Camphor-scented candles stand in basins of perfumed water. Each low table has dishes of betel nuts, cardamom and roasted coriander seeds.

The proceedings are formal, but under the refinement there is passion.
Some lines I noted down:

> *The boat has reached the shore: don't compain about the boatman.*

There was much about death, though the theme was supposedly movement as well as stillness.

> *Clothes can't hide the nakedness of night; only the shroud can do that*

and

> *I pray: let this be, or let that be – in case there be nothing.*

I think Zafar himself was responsible for one unsettling question:

> *If there was no death, where would be the charm of living?*

The poets sat in a circle, leaning on their richly upholstered *gao-takiyahs* (bolsters). The *chobdar** in green and gold carried the lighted *shama* from one to another. Its long flame bent or flounced dreamily.
The evening's final triumph was reserved for the renowned *ustad*, Mirza Asadullah Khan, whose pen-name is 'Ghalib'.

> *As the image of the bridge arch in the turbulent river dances,*
> *Discover delight in disaster, stand up yourself – and dance!*
>
> *There's no virtue in promise-keeping. If you're happy momentarily, take your luck.*
> *But if you make a promise and she thanks you – dance!*
>
> *The journey is its own reason; ending's not the point.*
> *So when the coachman rings his bell, don't stand and stare – dance!*
>
> *The garden was green with life when we walked its paths together.*
> *Round the corner the bonfire smoked, so, like the flame – dance!*
>
> *In the wastes of the desert no love's to be found;*
> *Copy the whirlwinding sandstorm – dance!*
>
> *Forget the old conventions, how 'polite society' works;*
> *Be glum at weddings, and at funerals – dance!*
>
> *O Ghalib, who shackles you to this exultation?*
> *Even when you're mouldering in prison* – dance!*

27 May 1857
On my way to a poetry evening, walking down Chandni Chowk, I notice: everyone animated, agitated.
News, news.
The news is of Indian soldiers rebelling against the British – a revolt, a defiance.
What will happen?

16 May 1859
With a heavy heart I resume my diary. But no time or place for poetry now.

The Indian soldiers who rose against the British have been defeated, roundly defeated, and humiliated.
What was Dehli is now a desert.
The people, the Moslems especially, have nearly all fled, or been driven out. The British put all the blame on the Moslems for the so-called 'Mutiny'. But there were just as many Hindus up in arms as Moslems. It's a wedge between old comrades. 'Divide and rule', I think they call it.
The places where some have stayed near the city are bitter, the people cold and hungry. They are not allowed back.
Perhaps the lucky ones were murdered. There were plenty of them. For days, the gutters frothed blood. Instead of people, we have a new population now – grief, despair, desolation, agony.
Parents have gone. Children ask their grandparents for a cup of milk. They get no reply.
The street sweeper, the *dhobi wallah*, the barber – all vanished. The shops are closed, deserted. There is no grain for bread. Water is scarce, sometimes there is no water for days together.
And the British loot. Their authorities encourage the looters. They hand out 'digging tickets' to those who wish to rob us.
Libraries which included handwritten collections of the poems of Ghalib, Zafar and others have been ransacked and utterly vandalised. The gold and silver tooling on spines and covers was manna for looters and scraped off. The contents of the books was of no interest – the defaced pages were torn to shreds, or burned, and thrown to the wind.
The Red Fort, the Emperor's palace, was despoiled and pillaged. Every gem and precious stone is gone, prized away by bayonet points. All the gold inlay has been torn out and stolen. The glass chandeliers were systematically smithereened.

The Emperor, aged 82, is imprisoned in a little dark cubbyhole. White people come to gawp and peer through the windowlet at him, sitting huddled on his bed.
Over Chandni Chowk and the Jama Masjid, silence hangs like smoke.

12 May 1862
I met Ghalib, the poet.
Once this would have been cause for excitement and rejoicing. How the vulture of time has picked our carcase.
He says, captivity is not a matter of bars or cages, but of your heart and your thoughts. 'I am merely one note in the symphony of eternity.'
He has suffered. He was himself, with his family, arraigned before the British. They failed to prove anything against him, though that was not enough to save many. Ghalib, however, was allowed home.
Not so Zafar. He was tried (they called it a trial, anyway) and sent into exile in Burma.
Ghalib watched the British take the city. They killed anyone they found out of doors. Mass arrests, killing, indiscriminate violence. People lost everything, except their honour – though many people lost that, too, especially women.
Chandni Chowk was a hangman's paradise.
Ghalib spoke of the famine of two years ago, too. How merchants hoarded grain and no-one forced them to sell to the starving people – just as in 1837. The British could have saved hundreds, thousands, of lives. They didn't.
Instead, they knocked down cherished buildings and left the people who were already starving, homeless.
They ignored the contaminated wells, too, and so let the Dehli sore, the fevers, and the spiteful, deadly cholera, scamper free like a hungry cat.
Ghalib looked grey, his cheeks hollow. He has written no poetry.
'Where is Dehli now?' he asked. 'Yes, there once was a city called Dehli ...'

15 May 1862
I have been told the most extraordinary thing about the fight some Indian people put up against the British five years ago. Whether to believe it or not I am uncertain.
I have been told that the bravest soldier who fought against the British was a woman.
The Ranee of Jhansi*. She was killed fighting.
Some strange happenings in our time. Has history stopped?
Some say that she was the incarnation of Mother Ganga, holy river, whose mission it was to cleanse our country. Others that she was an avatar of the goddess Kali, brought to earth to annihilate again in order to reveal the truth of things, to restore to us the spiritual strength the British have robbed us of.
She herself is supposed to have said that to defeat the British was her *dharma*.
What to make of all this, I am uncertain.

18 September 1862
No flower festival now. I was to meet Ghalib today. He did not arrive.
Famine hobbles hungry through the streets again.
Too much rain.
Flooding scuttles houses,
They flounder and sink
As if their walls were made of mud, wet mud.
Nothing to eat:
Death is cheap, grain dear.
Poverty never relents.
Big houses trample
On the space where once
The dwellings of the poor huddled.
There is no *chowkidar* to tap the street by night.
Burglars pad the pavements
As they will,
Make good their bad.
I hear of Hasan Ali Khan, the prosperous merchant we all knew.
His pension was

One hundred rupees a day. The British masters reduced it to
One hundred rupees a month. He is now
Dead,
In a pauper's grave.
And Agha Sultan was foolish enough to fall ill.
Medicine is at British prices now.
He, too, lies
In a pauper's grave
In Dehli,
City of the dead.

13 November 1862
Word has it – Zafar is dead.
At last.
He was bundled into an unkept grave in Burma
With horrid haste. So –
No quiet rest
In Qutd Sultan's *Durgah* plot,
For him
Only an unnamed smudge of earth.

I have been given a copy of one of his last verses:
> *Why seek a witness*
> *For what's happening?*
> *Hopelessness, O Zafar,*
> *Is its own witness.*

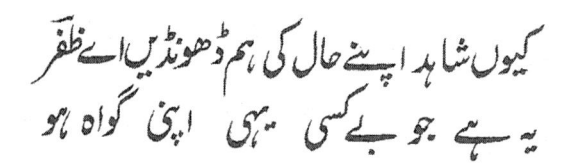

کیوں شاہد اپنے حال کی ہم ڈھونڈیں اے ظفر
یہ ہے جو بے کسی یہی اپنی گواہ ہو

Bahadur Shah II 'Zafar': original Urdu script of 'Why seek a witness'.

Ghalib didn't meet me. But he sent a poem:

The English soldier waggles his sword,
Struts the street, insolent, bored.

Life for those his eye descends on's cheap:
We cower, go by the wall, creep.

Chandni Chowk now tells a hangman's tale.
Your own house becomes your gaol.

Even the dirt on Dehli's streets seems to lust
To grind the Moslems into dust.

Going out or coming in's a forgotten dream:
We live, frozen in a scream.

You try to talk with old friends,
But tears and anguish is where it ends.

And it's not just show. We and this grief
Grow together, like tree and leaf.

The sky is shredded with despair;
Our cries echo in the cold, alien air.

Our life lies wounded, Ghalib, purple raw,
Pecked at, preyed on by a white jackdaw.

1 January 1863
O Ghalib, O Zafar, what is life
When there is no melody in the sitar
When there is no sweetness in the huqqa
When there are no dancing feet on the purple carpet
When there is no wine winking in the glass
         no head on my knee
         no gauze skirt swirling in the drifting incense

         no poetry

A City without Poetry

A city without poetry is a desert.
Compare the death of poetry with the loss of a lover.
There are pasts more pertinent than the personal.
Delhi deracinated. Could it ever recover?

Nationalist group at Ashoka's Stone, Delhi.

At Ashoka's Stone

'I am a nationalist, I believe
In the destiny of India,'
Urged the long-toothed man.
Then, sergeant-major-barking his slogans,
He flourished his right arm
At the green-and-orange national flag

And his comrades beyond
Flourished and barked in time.
It was
Soul-driven.
              It was
The climax of their ceremony,
Borne on the shoulders of a dozen
Stone-faced men ... which had begun with
The lighting of five soft-shaded candles
And the sweet chanting of a psalm-like song –
Statement – response; statement – response ...

But their meeting ground was no temple –
A little shed-like building
Enclosing rusty iron railings round
A scarred stone –
Ashoka's Edict –
Carved tablet from aeons past,
Chipped and cracked relic of
Perhaps a happier time. 'Now,'
The leader in his ruler-creased Viyella slacks
And smart pink shirt, its pockets lined
With silver pen-tops, snapped,
'People don't regard
The greatness of India.'

While his company
Shouted their adherence,
The little candles, one by one, were
Puffed out by the summer breeze.
The worn face of the old stone,
Bedecked with one or two dead lovers' vows
As well as ancient hieroglyphs,
Lay in sunlight
Striped by its cage's shadows.

The brotherhood of nationalists
Nodded fiercely to each other,
Shook hands, and

Departed for their mopeds,
While Ashoka's Edict
Went on silently proclaiming
The triumph of *dharma*,
The unity of people, the unity
Of all things. The afternoon hovered
Like a gnat in a shaft of sunlight.

I wandered into the nearby park,
Watched young men playing cricket –
'How's that?' – and pondered
The blossoming sales in India
Of *Mein Kampf.**

        *   *   *   *

We have lost the way. We're lost, realizing in self-disgust
The rivers of Delhi are not Ganga, not Karnali, will not lead
Where we are going. Better now to head
West, towards the lion, Indus, third of the four rivers in which
    we put our trust.

Seven : At Last

In Search of the Lion River

Kali-Shiva, bound blades,
Togethered, plough
Seeds of poetry, fuse
Dance, architecture, flame. Now

We must take breath.
We lost the way. Poetry
Is love-child of journey-imagining, not this
Political puppetry.

We must find
Renewal. Two ways – Brahmaputra, Ganga – lost,
Used up, like meadows mown,
Now stubble, sterile dust.

They promised repletion. Now we must add
New spices, herbs, to the already-feast,
Seek afresh a river, Indus, lion,
To relieve this desperate thirst.

Stop. Breathe. Can the old carthorse
Pull through? The course
Leads to Jaisalmer, desert city, last
Before moving west.

Sons of Sons of Khusrau

It was his eyes.
They clamped me like a padlock.
Specks of silver on the dark globes,
Lashes – brown reeds
In a spiteful blast.
He clutched my look in his.
Didn't answer. Just smiled.
Then went his way.

Five ragamuffin buskers had
Shuffled up to where we sat
Amid scraped bowls, wine bottles
Threequarters empty, a bill
As yet unpaid. Grandpa
On the one-string *sarangi**
Ground out a wavery bar or so,
And then
This boy's voice
Filled the evening, our heads,
The arc of everywhere
With high, plangent beauty,
And nothing mattered – only this.
Oh, if you could have heard
This boy turned bird ...
He overwhelmed infinitude!

After he'd sung, he smiled
With the arrogance of genius,
And toyed a little with his other skills:
Whistled airishly, clacked maracas,
Used his teeth to squeeze quivering melody
From his jew's harp ...
While grandpa fiddled, grinned
And folded, re-folded
Rupee notes his boy had won.
And three little brothers tumbled

In a bid maybe
To seem like dancers.

Eleven years old,
He told me. And —
The future? His eyes
Screwed mine tight
In a cousin of silence. Then
He snatched my proffered money
With a whisk of his head,
And made away,

And his voice
Filled the world vacuum
All evening long.

And I remembered
A few days earlier —
Stuck in traffic
My eye caught by
A boy with a drum, who
Dodged bikes, rickshaws, trucks to come near
And rat-tat outside my windscreen
On a talking tambourine,
And his brother, gaping, lop-side mouth,
Singing
Skinny, limpid lines.

I gave them rupees, too.
'Don't bother,' said the taxi man.
'They're Bangladeshis —
Refugees — beggars.'

But they also were
Sons of Khusrau,
Ghalib, Rabindranath Tagore,
And my pittance was my protest:
Artists of the pavement, they too
Whet our values.

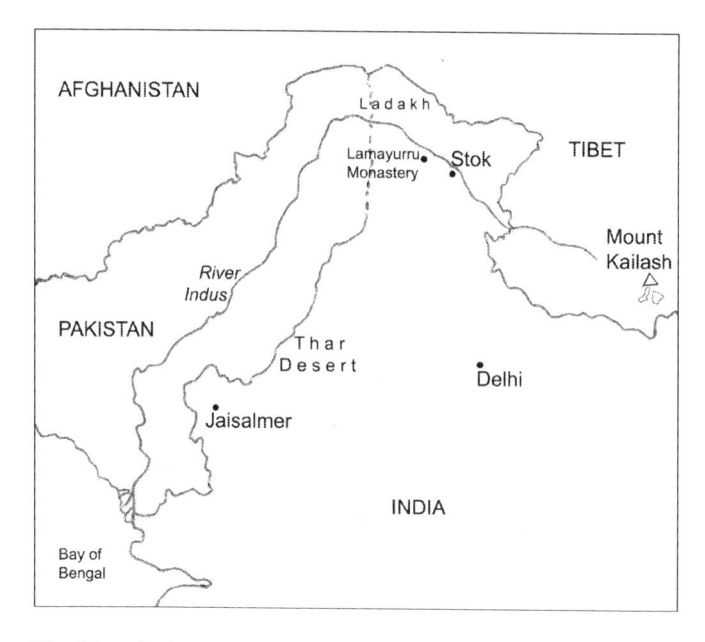

The River Indus

Through the Desert

Dust dry
Stone dry
Dry as blown sand
Only the camel can travel
In this dry land

The Thar Desert

The muffled thud of camel's feet
On naked sand, flickers of guttural encouragement
From the drivers, and the silence
Of bigness. Sky empty,
Vast blue dome
Battened down on every horizon.

We travel smooth
Across the musculature
Of dunes, strangers
In this strange land,
Sighingly
Through soft enticing curves,
The desert undressed,
Beige in the oven air,
Rippling away from us,
Gentling into gilded distance.

The camels wear
Red, green, blue rugs
Like frilly skirts.
Their walk is
Stately and ungainly,
They dawdle rapidly
Mile after mile.

Night still
Where we lie under a confetti of stars,
Wind unwhispered, sand
Unrustled – only
The flame of our own
Whirlwinding sandstorm
Waltzing
Past horizons of hours,
Past metre, reason, thought,

Till a slim plume of song
Spears up, pure like desire
In the dawn air,
Calling loud to god in the sky
– Our Moslem camel driver's
Morningly devotion
Opening his throat and heart.
And as dawn traces grey hatching across the tented void,
A bulbul atop a bush thrusts out his chest to add
His thin music to the virgin day.

We travel on –
Each rippling rise of ground
Round as woman's hip or breast,
The whole unrolled world
Beautiful and nude.

**The Desert Beetle Teaches the Sun a Lesson
in Self-Determination**

The desert beetle
The sand
The sand
The desert beetle
One in one, one becomes one
Solo soul
Needs no dune or bush or scraggy tree
Without leaves

The sand worm burrows and burrows
It extrudes
Curling strudels
Of dead sand

The passage way is dark
The steps
Perhaps
Worn
And that old conventional entranceway
Yawns

The beetle scurries towards an unknown hole, goes
Where the whim wills
Its tracks
Tiny courses in the sand
And soon the cruel simoom
Will dust them
To oblivion

And all the while
And as expected
The red sun tups the horizon
While all the rest of the high blank` sky
Is pure blue

On our journey
One horizon
Melts into
Another horizon

Everything changes

And all our wayside stops bestride
Meetings and partings
Goodbyes and deaths

Time dances
On the belly of eternity
While on the desert floor
The beetle
– Black round pod
On microscopic legs –

Goes on
Hurrying on
And on

And the wind wipes out what's gone

        *   *   *   *

Dust dry
Sand dry
Dry as white bone
Only the camel can travel
In this dry zone

        *   *   *   *

And then, like a high tide
Scaling a steep beach,
We've gone as far as we can. An
International border. So the River Indus, too, is out of our
    reach?

Pakistan –
Another partition
Bequeathed by
Britain.

Desert fruit,
Laughing in the red noon,
Promise of renewal a mere mirage,
Melts like a waning moon.

But
We will connect again.
Indus flows from the north, through north India.
We will connect.
We will not allow this barrier.

Making the Connection

The Traveller

We spend our lives in airport lounges
Drinking coffee from cardboard cups
And listening while alien people
Discuss, joke, argue in languages
As foreign as our home.

'She's going to Delhi, to hospital.
It's her finger – to be amputated.
It's been getting out of hand.' My imagination
Lifts off like a Kingfisher airbus.

'May I take my water bottle
On the plane?' 'Yes, provided
You don't squirt the pilot
Either on take-off or landing.' 'But the plane
Runs on petrol. Or doesn't it?'
'Aha!'

I am a tubular chair
I am a public notice in three different languages
I am the IndiGo jet liner diverted to Bhubaneshwar
I am the stranger who seems to accompany you
On your every journey
I am the stranger
The traveller
I am

*   *   *   *

We reach
High Lamayurru –
White washed, crimson painted
Monk's haven, cloud-besieged above Dah-Hanoo;
Journey's start for Milarepa*, magus.

Milarepa and His Man on the Climb to Lamayurru

Mule-head!
Why want to go
Where mules themselves
Would hardly dare?

The silk traders have a reason –
Money – profit – jingle jingle.
I understand that. But merely to be
Nearer God … !

No. But yes, he said.
So yes it is.
Fur-lined boots, mittens, coats,
And a bad-tempered grumble to go with.

Oh, he slapped my back,
Made to make a joke of it,
Swung into his high step.
But I sole-dragged, grudged.

Nearer God! Nearly nearer
God's enemy. Steep, steep
And God forsaken, surely. Sheer vertical rock
Chopped into by the rough road.

Breath gasped and puffy,
Meagre air. Workers blasting rock,
Hats pulled down, scarves pulled up:
Stared at with red-whipped eyes.

Half way I dragged at his elbow.
'Don't. Enough.' I pointed to
The waterfall turned to ice,
Snow streaks like tear trails.

He set on forward to
A spindly bridge,

Swinging like a hanged man
In the steely breeze.

He crossed, and every step
Speared fear. Then me,
Shaky shuffling, felt boots sliding
And my gloves slipping on the iced rope rail.

Till over – and a dizzy runaway
Of tatty prayer flags strung across
The mad moonscape we traversed.
And then at last – the lamasery,

And somewhere in the roof eaves
Up near God
A solitary monk
Chanting his mantra –

Repeating repeating
Something strange, wild,
And no-one listening
For all the world.

Lamayurru monastery, Ladakh.

The Race Up Mount Kailash
(*A tale of magic and suspense*)

Milarepa was a monk,
 A holy tantric Buddhist;
He practised esoteric wiles
 Deep in the mountain forest.

A hermit he, lived by himself,
 A cave his habitation,
Whose door he stopped with piled-up bricks,
 And sat in meditation.

One night this lama dreamed a dream –
 His childhood home burned down,
His mother, sister, homeless now,
 Their world turned upside down.

His hands tore down the brick-built door,
 And out of the cave he flew;
He told his master he'd got to go
 To his mother, and sister, too.

But Marpa, guru, held his arm,
 And said: 'Yes, go – don't wait;
But at every cave that you come to,
 Stop and meditate.'

Milarepa left Lamayurru,
 The lamasery in the sky,
With its whitewashed walls and dull red roofs,
 A wild look in his eye.

Across the Ladakh range he went,
 The Karakoram, too,
Then on to the Gangadise way
 To Qomalingamu*.

And at every cave, as he'd been told,
  He stopped to meditate,
Till he came at last to great Kailash
  And here he stopped to wait.

Here Naro Bong-Chung reigned supreme,
  The champion of the Bon:
A sorcerer, a holy man,
  Who stood and beat a gong,

Which sounded and resounded far
  And signalled for all to know
That a contest here was to be held
  Between him and his Tantric foe.

And terrifying and cruel the match:
  They traded fire and clay,
They conjured demons, drowned poor seamen,
  And curdled milk to whey.

But one could not yet best the other
  So a final trial was set –
Who first could reach Mount Kailash top
  The victor's palm would get.

Naro mounted his magic drum
  Whose beats shot him uphill,
While Milarepa just meditated,
  Eyes shut, and sitting still.

But just as Naro neared the top
  Milarepa stood up tall:
He leapt on a ray of the golden sun
  Which whisked him to his goal,

And set him on Kailash' stony top
  While Naro still climbed on
– And thus did Tantric Buddhism
  Annihilate the Bon.

Ladakh

The pace quickens. The pulse
Sings. For us, together, our destination is nearer.
The place, Ladakh, seems dead,
But within is energy. We salute spring. The way truly is
　　clearer.

Remembering Khajuraho, we determine to emulate the
　　Tantric sage: tramp
From high Lamayurru to the far soaring mountain range,
Across snow-raked ridges, ice-fast tops
Where winds bite, frosts slight and every sight is strange

To find the mountain we dream of,
The place we aim for,
Our *dharma*,
What we came for.

Spring Coming
(*The masked chaam* at Stok Buddhist monastery*)

Spring coming?
The way of escape, the way out of winter,
Drums and throbs in ears and eyes.
No night time elephant ritual this – dawn, blue sky,
And sun smacking foreheads, sculpting shadows
Kali-black – purity in a cobra's egg.
And ice? Winds that slice like glass? Is this
Spring?

In the eager emptiness
　　　　　　　　of the lamasery courtyard,
　　Yellow awnings,
　　　　　　flags and frills,
　　　　　　　　　　adorn the morning.

A cluster
        of windburned
                people
                      's forming:
Brothers,
        neighbours,
                grandmas,
                      tots,
In woolly skirts,
                padded jackets,
                      shawls
                            and hats.
Prayer wheels
            whirl,
                    kids
                        uncurl,
Wrinkles,
        wriggles,
                chins
                      and grins
Show us
    how
        to bring in
                Spring.

First, *kurumkuzhals*
                and long trombones
                          and drums
Welcome
        what's coming,
                and now
                      what comes –

Masked monks
            swishing
                    their deep fold
                            skirts,

Spring Festival at Stok monastery.

Lyrical
      satirical
                their movement
                              alerts
A world
      of wonder
              which prepares
                          to unfold
In masks,
      in miracles,
             in cracking
                      every mould.

There are dragons
            with swords,
                        slow-stepping
                                    lords,
Animals,
        criminals,
                Chinamen,
                        bards ...
Patiently
        the people
                wait
                    to see
Midgets
        and monsters
                    and fiddle-
                            de-dee.
Then come
        the jesters
                – old friends,
                            these –
Flinging flour,
        hopping happy,
                    a giggle,
                            a tease.
They swizzle
        and twizzle
                a hundred
                        fine toys,
Pluck hats
        off old heads,
                and chuck chins
                            of bold boys.
Then they flourish
        a red rag
                doll-on-a-string,
Who jigs up
        and jerks down –
                    a most
                        humanlike thing.

190

They each tug an end,
                    the doll
                              leaps
                                        high in the sky,

Somersaults,
            vaults,
                        lands in
                                    somebody's eye.
'Oops!'
        and 'Ooo!'
                        – this rag doll
                                        can't hurt a fly.

Then it gets serious.
To the ominous,
                    repetitive
                                trombone's
                                            'wurr',
The enemies
            of renewal
                        stir
                            and burr:
Theirs
      the energy of emptiness,
                                theirs
                                        the flag of fear,
Theirs
      the whisper
                  of without-ness
                                    in somebody's ear.
They flaunt,
            challenge,
                        run amok
And spectators
                flinch,
                        shuffle,
                                duck.

Footsteps
   fly,
     the chase
        is on,
They sprint,
    they scramble,
        spit
         and run
Up stairways,
    past watchers,
       along
         juddery gutters,

They're glimpsed
     in sun patches,
       through doorways
          and shutters.
Then
  on the rooftop,
      smashing
        flagpoles,
Disappearing,
    reappearing
       in unexpected
          portholes.
They breathe
    their death threats
        at all
         who boo,
Brandishing
    swords
       with much
         ado!
But the folks
    fling flour,
       honey,
         seeds,

Climax of the spring ceremony at Stok monastery

Till with yowls
         and cries
                which no-one
                        heeds,
They're hullaballooed,
              swatted,
                    brained
                          and caned,
Dashed
      and bashed,
             again,
                  again;
And pummelled
            and catcalled,
                    and driven
                          away
And positively
          Spring
                can return
                      today.

Thin Air

This is our way.
The monks' high jinks paint the world anew.
As we get near and nearer to Kailash,
We must stretch to screaming every thew and sinew.

When all's done, Indus marks the way.
Like a green snake draped across the landscape,
It cuts out of the cruel land
Its own path of escape.

Higher – and breath breaks. Together being unpicked.
Pages drop from the script.
The higher we go, the less air.
Concentrate: there's no relief from breathlessness anywhere.

Mother Assassin

We pant:
Can't. Cant!
Is it that
As we approach Kailash
The ground gets stonier,
The path
Lonelier,
That we go
Slow?

From here
Strike for Kailash? No.

The Himalaya in its uniform –
Grey, khaki, off-white –
Stands between,
Guards our target

As the multitudes of Indian soldiers
Guard the line.

A few steps
And we're exhausted,
The air – emaciated, thirsty.

Were the desert's sensuous curves
A mirage? Bone dry,
Stone dry, no way through.

Or is it that
Performing spring
Is not
The real thing?
The March-bright sun
A mare
For those who shivered
In Ladakh's blade-edge air?

India –
Mother, assassin.
The larder is naked,
The spice trays
Empty, the herb beds
Barren, dead.

We're stuck. We
Wait. We perform
Waiting. Today
I perform
Today.

– And poetry?
– And dance?
Too late.

Magpies in Ladakh

Ladakh is a desert,
But icy, and the air
Spare as a prairie dog.

Grey – fawn – grey – ash grey;
Rocks – pale yellow grey;
Tall skinny leafless poplars like maiden aunts;
Stone lines – field edges.
Still
In the drab endlessness
Some life
Grasps the thistle of being,
Something's breathing
By this precipice of life's end:
A congregation of rattling magpies.
Black-white, black-white,
They cock their heads, jump and scoot
From leafless bough to bough,
Then stream away
Over the grey brown land. Their tails
Trail after …

But as day
Sighs itself away
And snowed ridges
Fade into faint grey,
Even these
Staggering madmen
Diminuendo to naught.

At Last

1
Day floats off. Wind
Blows dust up – it flies
Low to the ground.
Pieces of litter skip and prance
As if alive.

Darkness comes.
Three or four needle points of light,
A pale window in silhouette,
And a gasp of silence.

I have not learned
Lung-gom,
The skill of breath.
I am not
Dancing.

Perhaps this
Is a little like dying –
No fear, but clutching
Air, grasping
At breath, head a vague
Ache, and people being
Nice, friendly ... Sly,
I glide away from
Awareness. Muscles slack, brain
Drained – a kind of
Consciousness at arm's length,
A drifting, drifting off ...

My eyes close.
I hold your hand.
I feel your fingers firm round mine,
And I know now
There'll be no
Renewing, I'll never reach

Mount Kailash,
Or Mansarovar,
Or anywhere.

Floating away,
Not even wanting
Focus ...

2
Who am I?
Part of something
I am
Part of something else,
The axle in the spiral
I am

Not Shiva, not
Atop the mind-blown mountain

We have done the journey
The journey is done
It was the journey
The journey

I am
The journeyer
I performed
The journey

Who am I?
I am
The nut man
Vijay
The yak's wool shawl seller
The boy singer in Jaisalmer
I rehearse them
In verse

And you
I rehearse you
And myself
I am
Of them
Of you
I am
What we are
Journeying
To our Kailash of the mind

      3
Mount Kailash –
Stone black, earth and ice –
Chimera,
Unexistable, non-being.

Dreams, stories,
A brain unraveling,
A poem travelling,
Feet step, the lotus
Waits by the wayside.

          Besides,
Were you not Kali,
Did not meeting you
Make nirvana,
Perhaps? Scraps
Of solace
On this gaunt crown:
The journeying –
Dharma burning?

Kailash – spur
Spiking the flanks
Of panting, sweat-frothing self-recrimination,
And hope.
And time –

A chain
On faulty sprockets.

There is no Kailash
But the Kailash of the mind.
And what's gone
Is gone:
So fiercely brain and spirit blaze,
So little left in hand:
Ash
Falling where the wind blows,
A beetle track
In the sand.

Desert beetle.

The End

Notes

One
Rangoli : picture created with powdered pigment dropped onto the road or pavement; may be an abstract design or a recognizable picture, and is usually associated with festivals and offerings to the gods. (See illustrations on pages 15 and 73.)
Brahma : Hindu god of creation.
Ravana : ten-headed demon; the villain in the Hindu epic, *The Ramayana*.
Grief : 'up to 10 pilgrims from across south Asia died (in June 2009) from altitude-related illnesses near sacred Mount Kailash'. *The Guardian*, 7 July 2009.
Bons : followers of the ancient pre-Buddhist Tibetan religion.
Shiva : Hindu god of destruction – and of much else, too. Today Shiva is generally regarded as the most powerful of the gods.

Two
Nautch : 'A kind of ballet dance performed by women; also any kind of stage entertainment.' Henry Yule and A.C.Burnell, *Hobson-Jobson*, Chennai: Asian Educational Services, 2006, p.620.
Mumtaz and *Shah Jahan* : Shah Jahan – Mughal emperor, reigned 1627-1658. His favourite wife was Mumtaz Mahal, whose death he commemorated by building the Taj Mahal for her mausoleum.
Murgh : chicken dish.
Ashoka : 3rd century BCE Buddhist Indian emperor, often regarded as India's most enlightened leader.
Aurangzeb : son of Shah Jahan and Mumtaz Mahal, who overthrew and imprisoned his father; emperor 1658-1707.
Simla and *Ooty* : summer capitals of the British raj. Ooty is the popular name for Udagamandalam.
Reds and colours : snooker was invented by the British in Ooty.

Mrs Hauksbee : a central character in Rudyard Kipling's *Plain Tales from the Hills*, set in Simla.
Dharma : the way to go in life; the forging of the unity of the soul.
Malabar : old name for the southern part of India's west coast.
Boxwallah : street hawker.
Puja : any kind of Hindu religious rite.
Divali : Hindu festival of light; also known as 'Kali puja' in honour of the goddess Kali. (For Kali, see notes to Five below.)
Babachee : cook; but also, anyone who deals in food.
Bhadrikali : a notably upbeat incarnation of the goddess Kali.
Cochin : old name for Kochi.
Tuk-tuk : auto-rickshaw.
'Though woe be heavy ...' : from William Shakespeare, *The Rape of Lucrece*.
Brain-fever bird : the hawk cuckoo, whose repetitive, annoying call is supposed to induce brain fever.

Three
Vahanna : quite roomy carriage carried by two or, more usually, four men, like a palanquin.
Lingum : Shiva represented as phallus.
Darshan : a glimpse of the god.
Today's rulers in Tamil Nadu : local politics in the state of Tamil Nadu has since the 1970s been bitterly split between the DMK party, fiercely Tamil nationalist, and the AIADMK, led by south Indian film superstars. Fraud and corruption, personal jealousies and an unscrupulous policy of jailing one's opponents has scarred and disfigured local politics for decades.
Builders' screens, coconut leaves : every eight or ten years, the fabulous towers of the temple at Madurai are re-painted. When this happens, they are screened off with coconut leaves so the painters can work in the shade. It seems a pity, however, that all four towers are screened off simultaneously.

Four
Yoni : female sexual organ.
Secrets in stone : Mamallapuram on the Coromandel coast is a World Heritage Site because of its stunning range of monuments dating from the sixth to the tenth centuries CE. These include stone *rathas* (temples in the form of chariots), *mandapas* (cave sanctuaries), the famous shore temple, as well as huge *bas reliefs* carved in granite rocks. Among the most brilliant are the Krishna *mandapa*, which contains astonishing carved images of Krishna's mythic life juxtaposed in a single long carved panel; the Mahishamardini cave, which includes a superb panel of Durga slaying the bull-demon, Mahisha; and the vast 'Arjuna's Penance' *bas relief*, carved on two adjacent boulders separated by a natural cleft, said to represent the river Ganga (Ganges).
Today at the site, wherever you go to see these wonders, you are approached by rickshaw drivers, all manner of hawkers, or indeed any locals, offering to show you the wonderful range of stone art works – for a few rupees, of course!
Krishna : flute-playing avatar of Vishnu (see below), perfect lover and exemplar of the Hindu concept of godly life.
Vishnu : the preserver god; with Brahma (the creator) and Shiva (the destroyer), Vishnu forms the most powerful trinity of Hindu gods.
Bhima ratha : temple (*ratha*), dedicated to Bhima, one of the Pandava brothers, and a hero in the Hindu epic, *The Mahabharata*.
Durga : one form of Shiva's consort, from whose forehead (according to one myth) Kali emerged; but according to others, Durga and Kali are alternative forms of the same goddess.
Mahisha : bull-headed demon who attempts to overthrow the gods, and is defeated by Durga.
Arjuna : one of the Pandava brothers, the hero of *The Mahabharata*. In the story, he did penance by standing on one leg for a year, in order to obtain from Shiva the invincible *pashupata* weapon.

Robert Houdin : nineteenth century French magician.
Bartholomew : old Edinburgh map-making firm, taken over by HarperCollins in 1989.
Theyyam : performance ritual of north Keralan villages, such as Kunnur.
Daria : probably a form of Darikan, the demon.
Elephant festivals : these are held in the temples of many towns and villages in south India. The poem is based on the festival at Vaikom.

Five
Harappans : ancient Indus civilization, dating from around 2500 BCE.
The fourth river : the fourth river is in fact Sutlej, but for a time it was thought to be the Hwang Ho.
Chowringhee : main street in Kolkata.
Bankim Chandra Chatterjee : Bengali novelist of the second half of the nineteenth century. He originated the slogan, 'Bande Mataram' ('Pray for the mother').
Kali : the special deity of Bengal and Kolkata. Her most famous temple in the region is in the district of Kalighat in south Kolkata. For more on Kali, see Ajit Mookerjee, *Kali: The Feminine Force*, London: Thames and Hudson, 1988.
Curzon : (1859-1925) Viceroy of India, 1899-1905.
Jyotindra Mohan Tagore : brother to Rabindranath Tagore.
Banglar mati Banglar jal : 'The soil and waters of Bengal'.
 Let the soil and the waters and the air and the fruits of
  Bengal be holy, my Lord!
 Let the minds and the hearts of all brothers and sisters of
  Bengal be one, my Lord! etc
See Krisha Dutta and Andrew Robinson, *Rabindranath Tagore, the Myriad-Minded Man*, London: Bloomsbury, 1997, p.144.
Chana sattu : roasted gram flour, softened and usually served with pickles and chillies.
The great tree : the great banyan tree in Kolkata's Botanical Gardens is reputedly the largest in the world, standing 24.5m tall with a circumference of 420m.

Robert Clive and the wealth of Bengal : when Clive returned to England in 1760, three years after the Battle of Plassey, he brought home with him £230,000 in Dutch bills, £41,000 in bills on the company, £30,000 in diamonds, £12,000 in other bills, and more. He claimed to be 'astonished' at his own 'moderation'. See Antony Wild, *The East India Company*, London: HarperCollins, 1999, p.95.

Communism in Kolkata and Bengal : The history of the Communist government of Kolkata from its bloody birth at the time of the Naxalite rebellion, c.1970, is constantly more complex – and interesting – than this perhaps naive encounter with it in 2009 suggests, for which I tender my sincere regrets to the citizens of this remarkable and resilient city. The contradictions may be illustrated by two quotations from Kolkata native, Krishna Dutta's *Calcutta, a Cultural and Literary History*, New Delhi: Roli Books, 2003. Page 191: 'the Left Front claimed to have intellectual and cultural aspirations, but their policies delivered little.' Page 196: 'There is no doubt that average seven-year-olds in Calcutta have far better literacy and numeracy skills than their British or North American counterparts.'

Sarani : Bengali word for 'street'.

Gorkhaland : many people in north Bengal want their own state, not ruled from Kolkata. Their name for such a state would be 'Ghorkhaland'.

Daba : restaurant.

Six

Benares : old name for Varanasi, in use in the British period.

Kashi : the oldest name for Varanasi, meaning light.

Chausath Yogini : ninth century temple, now in a sad state of disrepair, dedicated to Kali and her sixty-four 'yoginis', or attendants. Only thirty-five of the shrines – perhaps half the original number – remain, together with the central shrine to Kali herself. Not far away, perhaps significantly, the remains of a small contemporaneous temple to Shiva are to be found.

The moon scowled into the darkness : according to some versions, Mumtaz called Shah Jahan to her side when she

realized she was dying, and passed away gazing into his eyes. This version seemed to me impossibly romantic.
Barfi : Indian sweets made with nougat.
Sri Niwas Puri : pronounced 'Shrinny' (rhymes with 'skinny'), 'Vash' (rhymes with 'lash'), 'Poor-y'. 'Shrinny-Vash-Poor-y'.
Dhobi wallah : laundry man.
Chowkidar : night watchman.
Hazrat Nizamuddin : Sheik Nizam-ud-Din (1236-1325), Sufi mystic and fourth saint of the Chistiya Order. His mausoleum in east Delhi is a place of popular pilgrimage, and crowds throng there all the year round. Women are strictly forbidden to enter the inner shrine.
Amir Khusrau : real name Abdul Hasan (1253-1325), poet, songwriter, singer, musician, reputed to have invented the *sitar* as well as the favourite Urdu verse form, the *ghazal*. He worked to build bridges between the Moslem and Hindu communities, and was employed by several successive Delhi sultans as court poet and historian. A notable Sufi scholar himself, he became a disciple of Nizamuddin, and is buried in the same precinct. Some of his work is available on the double CD, *Hazrat Amir Khusrau*, Ninaad Music, Mumbai; www.ninaadmusic.com.
The river of love ... : quotation from Amir Khusrau.
Bahadur Shah II : (1775-1862) the last Moghul emperor, 'reigned' 1837-1858. In fact he wielded virtually no power, though he paraded through the streets of Delhi quite often, in some pomp, and lived in the Red Fort. He was acclaimed by the soldiers who led the 1857 rebellion as their emperor, and the British held him responsible, though he certainly had no real hand in any of the actions of the uprising.
Mushairah : 'A *musha'irah* is a poetic symposium, a soirée at which poets of the day read their original works for pleasure. A *musha'irah* is not an easy form of entertainment. It demands full intellectual and emotional participation within the prescribed framework of aesthetic conventions set by the masters long ago. In course of time *musha'irahs* became, in addition, excellent forums for literary criticism, disputation and, sometimes, on-the-spot poetic compositions. But the

main purpose of a *musha'irah* is to offer opportunities for the enjoyment of reciting and listening to selected *ghazal* poetry.' – Qamber, Akhtar, *The Last Musha'irah of Dehli*, New Delhi: Longmans Oriental, 1979, page 18.
Ustad : master poet.
'Vah vah! Vah vah!' 'Subhan Allah!' : 'Bravo! Well done!' 'God be praised!'
Dehli : Mughal spelling of the capital city. 'Delhi' is an anglicization.
Father of the Mughals : Hamayun, emperor 1530-1540 and 1555-1556. He was deposed, but later regained the throne. His tomb is one of the finest monuments in Delhi.
Safdarjung : (1708-1754) chief minister to the Moghul emperor, Mohammed Shah; his tomb is a magnificent baroque edifice, still a major tourist attraction.
Dargah : enclosed Moslem shrine.
Ghalib : real name Mirza Asadullah Khan (1797-1869), perhaps the greatest Indian poet of the nineteenth century. He is buried in the Nizamuddin precinct, where the Ghalib Academy is also situated.
Koochah : narrow street, or alley.
The people long to see the poets arriving : the night of a *mushairah* was almost like a modern film première in Leicester Square, so popular was poetry in Delhi at this time. According to *The Last Musha'irah of Dehli*, 'This was a golden age for Urdu poetry. Everybody from the king down to the beggar was smitten with the poetic craze.' (*op.cit.*, p.40)
Chandni Chowk : though the word 'chowk' really means a square, Chandni Chowk is Delhi's most famous thoroughfare, leading to the Red Fort.
Chobdar : usher, or bearer, who carries the *shama* from poet to poet.
Mouldering in prison : in 1847 Ghalib was arrested for gambling, and sentenced to a fine of 200 rupees and six months hard labour.
The Ranee of Jhansi : (c.1827-1858) the Maharanee of Jhansi, widow of the Maharajah of Jhansi in modern Uttar Pradesh, led the forces of central India against the British in

1857-8. A kind of Indian Joan of Arc, she died in battle after a series of stirring exploits. See D.V.Tahmankar, *The Ranee of Jhansi*, New Delhi: Rupa and Co., 2007.
Sales of 'Mein Kampf' : this book by Adolf Hitler sells more copies per year in India in the early twenty-first century than in any other country in the world.

Seven
sarangi : classical Indian stringed instrument.
Milarepa : Tantric Buddhist saint (c.1052-c.1135), who reputedly challenged the champion of the old Tibetan religion, Bonism, to a duel; his victory seems to symbolise the triumph of his version of Buddhism over the old religion, which however still clings on in a few parts of the interior of Tibet. His (perhaps apochryphal) autobiography is published: *The Life of Milarepa*, translated by Lobsang P.Lhalungpa, London: Penguin Compass, 1984.
Qomalingamu : Mount Everest
Chaam : festival performance by Buddhist monks in their lamasery, watched mostly by local people. As the spectacular nature of these performances has become better known, quite a few have been transferred from the end of winter to the tourist season in the summer. At Stok, however, the performance described here took place in the first week of March, still desperately cold even under a blue sky.

INDIGO DREAMS PUBLISHING
132 HINCKLEY ROAD
STONEY STANTON
LEICESTERSHIRE
LE9 4LN
UNITED KINGDOM
WWW.INDIGODREAMS.CO.UK